THE ROUNDABOUT

Gerri Hill

BELLA
BOOKS

2016

Bella Books, Inc.
P.O. Box 10543
Tallahassee, FL 32302

Printed in the United States of America on acid-free paper.

First Bella Books Edition 2016

Editor: Medora MacDougall
Cover Designer: Linda Callaghan

ISBN: 978-1-59493-520-6

Other Bella Books by Gerri Hill

Angel Fire
Artist's Dream
At Seventeen
Behind the Pine Curtain
The Cottage
Chasing a Brighter Blue
Coyote Sky
Dawn of Change
Devil's Rock
Gulf Breeze
Hell's Highway
Hunter's Way
In the Name of the Father
Keepers of the Cave
The Killing Room
Love Waits
The Midnight Moon
No Strings
One Summer Night
Paradox Valley
Partners
Pelican's Landing
The Rainbow Cedar
The Scorpion
Sierra City
Snow Falls
Storms
The Target
Weeping Walls

About the Author

Gerri Hill has thirty published works, including the 2014 GCLS winner *The Midnight Moon*, 2011, 2012 and 2013 winners *Devil's Rock*, *Hell's Highway* and *Snow Falls*, and the 2009 GCLS winner *Partners*, the last book in the popular Hunter Series, as well as the 2013 Lambda finalist *At Seventeen*. Gerri lives in south-central Texas, only a few hours from the Gulf Coast, a place that has inspired many of her books. With her partner, Diane, they share their life with two Australian Shepherd's— Casey and Cooper—and a couple of furry felines. For more, visit her website at gerrihill.com.

CHAPTER ONE

Megan rolled over and groaned, keeping her eyes firmly closed as the pounding in her head echoed loud enough for her to hear it. Her mouth was parched and she tried to swallow. She groaned again as the bitter taste of tequila lingered.

"Oh, God," she murmured. She had a vague recollection of holding a bottle of Patrón hostage most of the night.

Then her eyes popped open when she realized she wasn't alone in her bed. She turned her head slowly, seeing a mass of light brown hair spilled across the pillow.

Oh. Dear. God.

Who the hell was in her bed? Julie? *Oh, surely not.* She couldn't have been *that* drunk. Melissa? No, Melissa had dark hair, thank God. Her eyes widened again. Oh, crap. Was it Sarah? *Oh, please say it's not Sarah!*

She closed her eyes tightly. Who else had hair this color? Her eyes popped open again. Mary Beth? *Oh, just shoot me if it's Mary Beth!*

"Good morning, angel," came a raspy, sleepy voice beside her.

She turned her head slowly, unable to contain her gasp as she locked eyes with Mary Beth Sturgeon. Several seconds passed before she could find her voice.

"What the hell are you doing in my bed?"

Mary Beth smiled at her. "Your bed?"

Megan sat up as fast as her pounding head would allow. She groaned as she looked around.

"Oh, *God*, this isn't my bedroom." Then she groaned again. "*Christ*, I'm naked," she mumbled as she clutched the sheet to her chest. She looked over at Mary Beth and saw her bare shoulders. *Oh. Dear. God.*

She spotted her clothes on the floor beside the bed and she motioned to Mary Beth. "Turn around."

Mary Beth's smile was smug. Too smug, Megan thought.

"Too late for that," Mary Beth said. "I've already seen every inch of your beautiful body. More than once."

"Oh, crap," she murmured. She bit her lip, then flung the covers off. She quickly reached for her sweater and pulled it on, covering herself as much as possible. She snatched up her undershirt but couldn't find her bra or underwear in the two seconds she allowed herself to look for them. She yanked on her jeans, nearly falling as her left foot got stuck in the leg. She danced around, managing to pull them on. She finally zipped the jeans, then grabbed the bridge of her nose, trying to ease the pounding in her head. She looked at Mary Beth and gave her what she hoped was a threatening glare.

"Not...a...word of this to anyone," she said as she bent down to pick up her shoes.

Mary Beth laughed. "Seriously? Half the women in Eureka Springs want to sleep with you," she said. "You think that I'm not going to tell everyone that you shared my bed last night?"

Megan stared at her in disbelief. If she was ever going to sleep with someone in this town—and certainly Mary Beth Sturgeon wouldn't have even made her top twenty—she would at least hope she'd remember it. Instead of arguing, she held up her hand.

"I'm leaving." She turned and stormed from the room.

"I have an extra toothbrush," Mary Beth called. "And ibuprofen."

Megan stumbled out onto the front porch, immediately shielding her eyes from the sun. What in the hell happened last night?

Well, it was her birthday. She remembered that much. And yeah, Nancy—her sister—had thrown her a party. She nodded. Yeah…at Mary Beth's house. It was supposed to be a surprise. She hadn't had the heart to tell Nancy that she'd known about the party for the last three weeks.

"Tequila? Who the hell brought Patrón?"

She looked around for her car, not seeing the black SUV anywhere on the street, which meant Nancy drove it home.

"And she freakin' left me here with *Mary Beth Sturgeon*? I'll kill her."

She paused on the street, squinting. Mary Beth lived above town, a couple of blocks from the business district. She looked uphill. The house she shared with her sister was four or five blocks away. She sighed and looked down the hill. She wanted coffee. She could walk to the grill for that. But she really wanted a shower and a change of clothes too. She glanced up the hill and sighed again. Two blocks downhill for coffee or five blocks uphill for a shower?

Downhill and coffee won.

As she headed down the street, she reached in her jeans pocket for her phone. A moment of panic set in when she couldn't find it. She couldn't *live* without her phone. Was it at Mary Beth's house?

"Oh, hell. I don't need my phone that badly," she murmured as she continued down the street.

"Hey, Megan. Great party last night."

She looked across the street, seeing Paul waving at her. Or was he laughing at her? She forced a smile to her face and returned the wave. She had no recollection of Paul even being at the party. Of course, she didn't have much recollection of the party at all. Which, at the moment, was the least of her worries. It was obvious that she was coming from Mary Beth's house. Paul would tell Michael. Michael would tell Steve. Steve would be on the phone to Carla in a matter of seconds. Carla would tell Susie. And Susie? Susie owned the corner grocery store on Main Street. The store that all the locals used. And Susie was the town's biggest gossip. If you wanted to know anything that was happening in Eureka Springs, you called Susie.

"Just freakin' shoot me already," she mumbled.

As the Phenix Grill came into sight, she picked up her pace. She had no idea what time it was but judging by the number of cars, they were already open and the lunch crowd was starting to trickle in. She walked inside, heading straight for the coffee. When Eileen would have spoken, Megan held up her hand and shook her head slowly.

"Don't...speak."

"Oh, that's right," Eileen said. "Tequila is not your friend."

Megan glared at her, but it had no effect on the waitress, who only laughed, grabbed the decaf decanter and sauntered off. Eileen had been with them since they'd opened the grill. That was the only reason she didn't fire her. Well, that, and the fact that she managed the waitstaff and they would be completely lost without her.

She skirted the kitchen and went directly to the office she shared with her sister. She plopped down in the chair, glaring at Nancy.

"Well, well. So you *are* still alive. Good."

"Why in the hell did you leave me there? With Mary Beth, of all people," She shook her head. "*Really?* What were you thinking?"

"You were asleep on the sofa, mumbling some nonsense about a circus clown. You told me to leave you there," Nancy said.

"The sofa? I woke up in her bed, for God's sake!"

"Well, yeah. We didn't want to leave you on the sofa. The party was still going on," Nancy said. "Paul helped us get you to her bed. I suggested the spare room, but Mary Beth thought you'd be more comfortable in her king bed."

"Oh, God, so Paul *was* laughing at me," she murmured as she closed her eyes. "I woke up *naked*. In Mary Beth Sturgeon's bed. And she was also *naked*." She groaned. "And I couldn't find my bra and underwear. My favorite bra…that cute little red one." She covered her face with her hands. "Oh, *God*. Now Mary Beth has it."

Nancy laughed. "Oh, Megan, Mary Beth was just having some fun. Trust me. There was no way you had sex last night."

"Fun? I wouldn't be surprised if there are naked photos of me posted on her Facebook page already," she said. She grabbed her head. "Oh, *God*. Mary Beth Sturgeon, of all people." She again glared at Nancy. "What were you *thinking?*"

Nancy waved her hand at her. "You're being way too dramatic. Mary Beth likes to pretend she's slept with everyone in town."

"That's because she *has* slept with everyone in town," she snapped. "And now they're going to think I've been added to the list."

"Everyone knows how you are, Megan. I'm sure they'll know better. But Susie was at the party…no telling what gossip is going around town already."

"Are you trying to make me feel better or worse? And where's my phone?"

Nancy reached for her purse and dug inside, coming out with Megan's phone. "You can thank me later," she said as she handed it to her. "Do you remember anything that happened last night?"

Megan frowned. "Well, it was my birthday."

Nancy nodded. "Thus the reason for the party."

"You do remember that I hate surprise parties, right? And if you're going to throw me one, why do it this year? I'll be forty next year. That should be the dreaded surprise party birthday."

"Because you would be expecting it at forty. Thirty-nine was a surprise." She raised her eyebrows. "Right? You were surprised, weren't you?"

Megan smiled. "Yes, I was surprised," she lied. "And paybacks are hell. You'll be fifty in a couple of years."

"Three. And don't remind me."

"So why did you take my phone?"

"To save you the humiliation you were about to incur." Nancy pointed at the phone in question. "You do remember the call, right?"

Megan frowned again. What call? She turned her phone on, going to her recent calls. Her eyes widened.

"Oh, my God. The Wicked Witch called? What the hell?" She looked at Nancy. "Did I talk to her?"

"No. I at least stopped you from answering. You did, however, listen to her message."

Megan nearly slammed her coffee cup down. "She breaks up with me on my birthday last year—in front of her new lover, no less—and she has the nerve to call me *this* year and wish me a happy birthday?" She narrowed her eyes at Nancy. "She did call to wish me a happy birthday, right?"

"In a roundabout way, yes. She was going on and on about how great this last year has been for the both of them and that she hopes you're finally over her and blah, blah, blah," Nancy said with another wave of her hand. "Your night went downhill from there. I don't know why you're not over her already."

"I am *so* over her," Megan insisted.

"Oh, yeah? Then why did you try to drink an entire bottle of tequila by yourself?"

Megan groaned. "I don't even like tequila. I don't ever want to see tequila again."

Nancy rolled her eyes. "You love margaritas, Megan. I'm sure this will pass."

"You took my phone. I was going to call her, wasn't I?"

"Yes, you were."

She sighed. She hadn't spoken to Erin even once since she'd walked out of her life. Erin had wanted to remain friends.

La Grange Public Library

Title: Murder is no accident
Item ID: 31320004614579
Date due: 6/20/2017,23:59

Title: The Roundabout
Item ID: 31320004622549
Date due: 6/20/2017,23:59

Title: Murder at the courthouse
Item ID: 31320004622598
Date due: 6/20/2017,23:59

Title: If not for you : a novel
Item ID: 31320004630690
Date due: 6/6/2017,23:59

Erin's new girlfriend wanted to be friends too. Megan wanted to shoot them both. Thankfully, they'd left town shortly after the breakup and Megan was saved from a murder conviction.

"Thank you. God only knows what I would have said to her."

"You're welcome." Nancy leaned her elbows on the desk. "Now, what do you think about the bookstore finally selling?"

"What are you talking about?"

"I swear, do you remember anything from last night? It was all the talk."

"The bookstore? Next door? It's been vacant for a few years now," she said. "Who would buy that dump?"

"Susie only knows it's some woman from California. Rumor has it that she's going to convert the upstairs into an apartment and live there."

Megan shook her head. "A plain old bookstore is not going to go over. Nobody reads paper books anymore. When Mr. Carlton owned it, even adding the little coffee bar didn't help."

"No, I doubt it'll be a bookstore," Nancy said.

"Well, I imagine we'll meet the new owner soon enough," she said. "And if you don't need me, I'm going home to take a shower and change clothes."

"It's your turn to close tonight," Nancy reminded her.

"Yeah, yeah," she murmured. "I'll be back at two."

CHAPTER TWO

Leah led the contractor back downstairs, pleased that he thought he could salvage the plumbing. Many, many years ago, the upstairs had housed two small apartments. The previous owner had gutted it and enlarged his bookstore, making the top floor a reading room. *Crazy concept*, she thought. No wonder the bookstore had failed. If you could spend a couple of hours sitting up there reading, why bother to buy the book?

"I want all of the shelves down here taken out too," she continued. "And as I mentioned on the phone, there's got to be more windows. It's as dark as a dungeon in here."

Mr. Holland walked over to the front wall and pounded against it with his fist, "I'd almost guess that there used to be windows here and they were closed up," he said. "Probably needed more shelf space."

"Unbelievable," she muttered.

He shrugged. "Everybody's got different ideas. Had an old house up above town. All original woodwork inside. Beautiful stuff. The new owner wanted something more modern though. Had me tear it all out and start over. Nearly made me cry."

"Well, I hope you salvaged it, Mr. Holland."

He winked. "I sure did, Ms. Rollins. And you can call me Tony. You got me looking around for my dad with all that Mr. Holland stuff."

She smiled and nodded. "Thank you. And please call me Leah."

"Yes ma'am. And like I said, we can get started on this next week. Got a remodel job over on Mill Hollow Road that we're finishing up. We can be out here bright and early Monday morning."

"That's wonderful, Tony. And you really think you can have the upstairs ready to go in only a few weeks?"

"As long as we don't hit any snags, yeah. Bedroom walls shouldn't take long. Bathroom and kitchen will be the most time-consuming, obviously, but if we don't have much wiring to redo, then, yes, a few weeks. Four at the most, I'd think. Then we'll be ready to start down here."

"Thank you. I'll plan accordingly. Appliances are already ordered."

He took his cap off and scratched his head. "I understand you're staying at the Howells' B & B over on Cliff Street."

She nodded, wondering how he knew that. Of course, she'd been warned by the real estate agent that it was a small, cliquish town. Since there were only two thousand residents, she imagined not much escaped notice.

"Not any of my business, of course, but staying there for three or four weeks, that'll run you a nice tab," he said.

"That's true," she said with a smile. "What? Do you have an alternative?"

"Well, my partner owns a couple of cottages that he rents out by the week. Tourist season won't pick up for another month—the Diversity Weekend, first week in April. I'd say he would cut you a deal. Certainly cheaper than the Howells," he said.

"I chose it because it's only a couple of blocks from here," she said. "I like to ride my bike."

"I understand. His cottages are up above town. Got a great view from them though."

"Well, thank you for the offer, but I guess I'll stay put."

"Okay, sure. Well, I'll see you Monday morning then."

"Thank you, Tony," she said as she followed him to the front door. "Oh, by the way. I noticed there is a 'reserved' parking sign out front here. I had assumed it was from the previous owner, but there's been this black SUV parked there."

"Oh, yeah. That's Megan," he said.

She frowned. "Megan?"

"She and her sister own the grill next door. Best burgers in town. You should try them. And they make a mean chicken-fried steak too."

She stood at the door long after he left, trying to decide what to do. She should just go next door, introduce herself, and ask this Megan person not to park there anymore. Yes, that's what she should do.

She looked around, seeing all the countless things that needed to get done before the remodel could take place. She couldn't believe how much junk had been left in the store. She should have hired someone to clean it out, but she reasoned she had the time to do it herself. Well, to box it up, at least. She would have to hire someone to haul it off.

She glanced back outside. Deciding that she didn't want to take the time to go next door, she went into the back room, found some paper and quickly jotted down a note. Then she went outside and pulled off the tacky, hand-made "reserved" sign that was fastened to a light pole. She then quickly stuck the note on the windshield of the SUV.

"There," she said. "That was easy."

She left the door open when she went back inside. It was a warm day, hinting of spring, and she hoped the breeze would chase out some of the musty odors. She'd been in town for eight days already, and this was the first warm day they'd had. The place had been closed up for over two years and as she started pulling old magazines off a shelf, she wondered—for at least the hundredth time—whether she was making a mistake or not. Oh, she didn't regret quitting her job. She'd been feeling stagnant for the last couple of years anyway. But why not retire and travel? Why not find a beach somewhere to sit on?

Because fifty is too damn young to retire, she told herself.

But not too young to quit a job she'd long grown tired of. She'd been in the tech industry her whole life, following both of her parents into the business. She'd written more damn code than she cared to remember. But it paid well and she never had the itch to quit, no matter how small her cubicle got.

Not until Aunt Ruby died, that is. Aunt Ruby was her father's aunt. The old maid of the family...a spinster woman. She grimaced as she remembered her grandmother's description of Ruby. She was far from a spinster, she thought with a smile.

When she was younger, she saw Aunt Ruby a few times a year, mostly during the holidays when her parents loaded them up for a week's stay in Los Angeles. As everyone got older, the visits got fewer and fewer, yet she and Aunt Ruby had formed a bond. It wasn't until she was in college—and out herself— that Aunt Ruby found the courage to confess to Leah that she was a lesbian. Leah had always suspected but had never mentioned it to her parents. Ruby had asked that she keep her secret and she had. As far as she knew, Ruby took that secret to her grave at the age of ninety-one.

But there was also another secret she'd kept from everyone, including Leah. She bought old houses, fixed them up, rented them out for a while, then sold them for a nice profit. Who would have ever guessed that Aunt Ruby flipped houses? And who would have ever guessed that Aunt Ruby was loaded?

Leah laughed quietly. And who would have guessed that Aunt Ruby would name Leah as her sole beneficiary? Certainly not her brothers or her parents—they'd been shocked to learn that she and Ruby had remained close. And certainly not her cousins. They couldn't even be bothered to go to the funeral, yet they were pissed as hell when they found out about the money. So pissed, in fact, that they had threatened a lawsuit.

That went nowhere, of course. But she wasn't exactly on speaking terms with them now. Not that they'd ever been close, she reasoned. She was lucky if she saw them once a year as it was. Oh, but money did crazy things to people.

She smiled and shook her head. Yeah…old Aunt Ruby was loaded, all right. Who knew she had a knack for California real estate?

CHAPTER THREE

"Steve says she's staying at the Howells'. Tony confirmed it."

Megan bit into her sandwich as her sister continued.

"And she rides a bicycle all over town. Susie says she even rode it up to Pivot Rock one day."

"So maybe she likes to exercise," Megan said. "I heard she was old though."

"Old? How old?"

"Totally gray-headed. Too old to start a new business, don't you think?"

"Who told you that? Tony met with her this morning. He's going to do her remodel. Steve didn't indicate that she was old."

Megan shrugged. "Just telling you what I heard." She couldn't understand what all the curiosity was about. So a new shop owner was in town? That happened all the time. Apparently, not with as much secrecy as this one though. Even Susie didn't know all the details yet.

"Maybe she's like Anderson Cooper."

Megan stared at her blankly. "What are you talking about?"

"Her gray hair. Maybe she turned gray early. Susie says she's really cute. Like *really* cute."

"Susie thinks everyone is cute. And what's with all the speculation about her? She's all people are talking about."

"New blood in town," Nancy said with a grin.

"Oh, my God. You don't even know how old she is or whether she's single or not. You don't even know if she's gay."

"Of course she's gay. Susie said she was."

Megan rolled her eyes. "Susie thinks *everyone* is gay."

"Do I have to remind you that nearly half of the people who live in this town are gay?"

"No, you don't. With all of the big old gay drama that goes on, no one should need reminding."

Nancy laughed. "Are you referring to Mary Beth?"

"Of course I'm referring to Mary Beth," she snapped. "It's been three weeks. She *still* has my picture on her Facebook page."

"At least the sheet was covering you. You can't even tell it's you."

"Really? Then why are people asking me if we're dating?"

Nancy laughed again. "It'll blow over. It always does."

"Yes, but no matter how much I deny it, they all think we slept together. And Mary Beth smiles in that smug way of hers just to keep everyone guessing. It drives me crazy."

"Which is why she keeps doing it. If you'd talk to her about it, have a laugh with her, it would all be over with already."

"Seriously? A laugh? She stripped me naked against my will!" she said loudly. "She took *pictures*!"

"Oh, God, Megan. Get over it already. That's old news."

"I wonder if you'd think it was old news if it was *your* picture on her Facebook page," Megan said pointedly.

"Then quit going out there and looking at it."

"I kept going out there to see if she ever took it down."

"And to leave comments. You forced her to block you and unfriend you. You were getting out of control."

Megan stood up and pointed her finger at Nancy. "I can't believe you are taking her side."

"Whatever. Get over it."

Megan shook her head. "I was over it. You had to bring it up again." She picked up her purse. "I'm going home."

"It's Friday," Nancy reminded her.

"I know. I'll be back by four."

They took turns opening and closing during the week, but on Fridays and Saturdays, they shared the duties. The tourists were only starting to trickle in, but the locals kept them plenty busy on the weekends.

She walked out into the sunshine, pausing to look up into the clear, blue sky. It had been cloudy and rainy for the last week so the sun was a welcome sight. She walked down the street to where she parked her SUV and got in. As she started it up, she noticed a note stuck under the wiper. She tilted her head, trying to read it.

"What the hell?"

She got out and yanked the note off, her eyebrows drawing together as she read it again.

I believe this parking space is designated for my shop, not the Phenix Grill. Please kindly park somewhere else.

"What the *hell*?"

Turning, she found the door to the bookstore standing open. Without thinking, she marched inside, holding the note up in the air.

"Who do you think you are?" she demanded.

The woman turned, surprise showing on her face. Then a smile appeared and she held her hand out in greeting.

"I think I'm Leah Rollins," she said.

Megan stared at her hand, then ignored both it and the easy smile the woman sported. "And this?" she asked, waving the note at her.

"Oh. Well, that's a note. I thought it was obvious."

Her tone indicated that it was a stupid question, and Megan found herself scowling.

"Yeah," the woman continued. "I left it for the person who's been parking in front of my store in that gas-guzzling SUV. There was even a 'reserved' sign there too." She scratched the back of her neck. "Was that you?"

"I'm Megan Phenix," she said through clenched teeth. "I own the grill next door."

"Oh...Phenix Grill. Huh." The woman smiled again. "I thought you'd just misspelled Phoenix."

"Ha ha," Megan said humorlessly. "And what do you mean, gas-guzzling? My SUV is midsized. It's quite conservative."

"Conservative? No. A hybrid would be conservative."

"Oh, my God. Are you one of *those*?" She shook her head. "Of course you are. You're from California."

Leah's eyebrows shot up. "Excuse me?"

"What do you drive? A Prius? Or a Tesla or something?"

Leah smiled. "Why, yes. I do own a Tesla. Electric cars are the future."

"Give me a break," Megan muttered. She held the note up once again. "Back to this," she said. "What is this all about?"

Leah gave her a puzzled look. "I thought the note was very clear."

Megan sighed. "Look, we've got the most popular eating place in town. In fact, you may have noticed that we're...we're just *packed* every night. And lunch. Even lunch too."

"Well, congratulations."

Megan ignored her patronizing tone. "You know, parking is really limited in town."

"Yes, I've heard that. I hear the lots down below town make a killing on parking."

Megan narrowed her eyes. "You're missing my point."

"You have a point?"

Megan blew out her breath. "My point is, shops that aren't busy *expect* other shops' customers to park there."

"Expect? It's my understanding that every shop has designated parking spots. Kinda like guaranteed spots," Leah said.

"Well, *technically*, that's true. But there's an unwritten rule about that. For example, say…your place here. You're not busy. But us? We're booming over there," she said, pointing out the door. "So you've got five parking spaces here not being used. It just stands to reason—common courtesy, if you will—that our customers would be allowed to park here."

Leah nodded. "Yes, that makes sense. But what if I have a customer come to my store and all of my parking spaces are full with your people? I'm going to lose business."

Megan looked at her incredulously. "You're not even *open* yet!"

"Well, I will be by summer."

"*Summer?*"

"Yes. Now's a good time to get used to not having these parking spots."

"Seriously? You won't be open until summer and you want to hoard these spaces *now*?"

Leah smiled at her. Megan perceived it as a condescending smile. That caused her to wad up the note and toss it—yes—childishly at the woman. She turned on her heel and strode purposefully out the door.

"Nice to meet you," Leah called after her.

"Insufferable woman," Megan muttered as she climbed into her car. "Cute, my ass."

CHAPTER FOUR

"The nerve! Can you believe it?"

"Well, it was kinda ballsy of you to put the reserved sign up in the first place," Nancy said.

"Mr. Carlton didn't have a problem with me parking there," Megan reminded her.

"That's because you brought him lunch most days. And you flirted with him."

"I did not flirt with him. He was old enough to be our grandfather."

Eileen stuck her head in the office. "Just a heads-up...Brent called in sick."

Megan groaned. "It's my turn, isn't it?"

Nancy smiled sweetly at her. "Yep."

"I *hate* waiting tables. Everyone knows we own the place. I swear, I get no tips."

Nancy waved her complaints away. "So...back to the woman. Was she cute?"

"I was too angry to notice if she was cute or not," Megan said, which was mostly the truth. She did, of course, recall the woman's easy smile. At the time, though, all she wanted to do was to smack that smile off her face.

"How old was she?"

"I didn't ask."

"God, you're so difficult," Nancy muttered. "Can you at least take a guess?"

Megan gave her an evil smile. "Seventy-five."

Nancy's eyes widened. "Seventy-five? Are you kidding me?"

Megan shrugged. "You said to guess." She got up. "I'll switch with you. I'll take bar duty, you wait tables," she offered.

"As much as I hate bartending...no," Nancy said.

* * *

"If Brent shows up tomorrow, he's so fired," Megan said to Eileen as she maneuvered her serving tray between two crowded tables.

"He's got the flu," Eileen said. "Give him a break."

Megan balanced the tray on one arm and forced a cheerful smile to her face. "Now...who had the buffalo burger?"

"Rare. I want it very rare," the man reminded her for the third time.

What? Is he a vampire or something? she thought. But the smile remained as she placed the plate in front of him, and she was pleased to notice a pool of blood next to the bun. Rare. Very rare. Very disgusting.

"Just as you ordered it, sir," she said cheerfully. She turned to the woman sitting next to him. "And for you, the spicy chicken burger with chipotle mayo on the side, as requested." Between them, she put a large platter of onion rings, then stepped back. "Anything else for you? Can I bring you another beer?"

They both nodded and she turned, nearly bumping into Trish as she passed by with a tray of draft beer and margaritas.

"Sorry," she whispered as the beer spilled over.

She hurried to the bar where Nancy was helping with the Friday night crowd. She waved her hand. "Need two Bud Lights here, lady," she called.

"Wait your turn," Nancy shot back.

Megan took a moment to exhale and look around. They were crowded, as they usually were on Friday nights, but there was a different buzz in the air. Perhaps it was the warm spring day they'd had. Or perhaps it was the anticipation of the fast-approaching tourist season. She saw strangers in the crowd— tourists—but mostly familiar faces, the local crowd who hung out there. Most of them, like she and Nancy did, made their living off the tourists who flocked to the Ozarks—spring, summer and fall and even up until the holidays. January and February were the dead months—except for the annual Mardi Gras celebration in February. Things slowed down then and it was a time for the locals to reflect on the past season, plan for the next one and take a few weeks to relax. During those months they closed the grill on Mondays and Tuesdays, their only true days off during the year. Things started picking up in March, starting with the St. Patrick's Day Parade. April, though, was the real beginning of the new season, when the trees began showing off their new green and the days warmed. More and more tourists would begin filling the streets then. And April, she reminded herself, was right around the corner.

"Here you go," Nancy said, sliding two frosty mugs her way.

"Thanks."

"Any tips yet?"

Megan nodded. "Yeah, Paul and Michael came in. They tipped me a whole buck."

Nancy laughed. "That's my boys."

Megan smiled back at her, then headed off to deliver her beer. It was a lively crowd this evening, conversations and laughter loud enough to drown out the music playing. She placed the beer next to the man and woman and stuck around only long enough to ask if they were enjoying their meal.

"The burger is perfect," the man said. "Excellent, in fact."

"Thank you. I'll be sure to pass on your compliment."

She turned to another table—a woman sitting alone still glancing through the menu. She was about to walk over when she stopped. Oh, crap, was it *her*? The woman had her back to Megan, but still, the gray hair looked too familiar. She glanced around, waving at Eileen. She then pointed at the table, silently asking her to take it. Eileen smiled and promptly ignored her, going to another table instead.

"I swear, she thinks she owns the place," Megan muttered.

She took a deep breath, plastered a smile on her face and went over to the table. If it was her, she would simply pretend she didn't recognize her and go on about her business.

"Welcome to the Phenix Grill," she said as she placed a drink napkin in front of her. "Can I get you something to drink or are you waiting for someone to join you?" she asked in her most pleasant voice. Her smile faltered, however, when the woman—Leah Rollins—looked up and met her gaze. Her eyes were a smoky gray, almost the same color as her hair. When she'd first seen her in the bookstore, she would have sworn her eyes were blue.

"Hello, Megan," Leah said, her glance traveling slowly over her, top to bottom. "Owner and waitress…that's admirable."

Megan didn't know why she felt the need to explain, but she did. "We're busy and shorthanded," she said, her words a bit clipped.

But Leah's smile was genuine. "I meant no disrespect, Megan. When I open my store up, I only hope I can afford employees," she said easily. "I may be doing everything myself."

Despite her smile, Megan refused to warm up to her. "So? A drink? Appetizer? Order to go?" she asked pointedly.

Leah laughed. "Wow…subtle. I see you're still pissed about the parking." Leah made a show of looking over her shoulder, as if assessing the parking situation outside. "As I walked over, I couldn't help but notice that all of my spots were filled."

"You're not even open yet!" Megan said through clenched teeth.

"I thought we'd covered that already."

Megan stared at her. *God, why does she keep smiling at me? I just want to smack her!*

But no. She could do no such thing to a customer. She squared her shoulders and tried to force a smile to her face. It just wouldn't happen for her though. *Screw it*, she thought.

"So…kinda busy here. Are you ready to order or not?"

"Well, I've been told by three people so far that you have the best burgers in town. I thought I should try one." She glanced at the menu. "You have so many choices though. What do you recommend?"

Really? *Really?* Megan sighed. "Without knowing your preferences, it would be hard for me to recommend one."

"My preferences, huh?" Leah asked, arching an eyebrow. "What would you like to know? If I like spicy or not?"

Megan stared at her. *Is she actually flirting with me? Seriously?* She shook her head. No, surely not.

"If you like spicy, I recommend the fiesta burger," she said evenly. "It has guacamole, pico de gallo, pepper jack cheese," she said. Then she smiled and added, "And healthy stuff like lettuce and spinach."

"Well, I was leaning toward the pesto burger because I love grilled zucchini and peppers and the garlic pesto sounds intriguing," Leah said.

"Also a good choice," she said.

Leah met her gaze. "But I like spicy. I'll go with the fiesta burger."

Megan nodded. "Rare, medium or well done?"

"Medium well, please," Leah said. "And I was also told your onion rings should not be missed."

"Yes, they are a local favorite," she said. "Regular or spicy?"

Leah laughed. "If we're going spicy all the way, I think I'll need a beer. Anything light. I'm not choosy."

"Coming right up," she said, turning to make a hasty exit to drop off the order. God, how could the woman be annoying one minute and pleasant the next? That, in itself, was infuriating. And flirting with her? *Really?*

"Why the frown?" Nancy asked as Megan leaned against the bar.

"That *woman* is here," she said. "And she's…she's annoying."

Nancy's eyes lit up. "Really? She's here?" Nancy scanned the crowd. "Where?"

"What is your obsession with her?"

"I just want to meet her, that's all."

Megan smiled. "Great! Then I'll let you bring out her dinner. In fact, she wants a light beer. You can take that to her," she said. "It's time for my break."

"Wait…you don't get a break," Nancy said. "It's Friday night."

"So fire me. She's at table twelve."

CHAPTER FIVE

Leah sipped from the water glass that had been placed in front her and absently scanned the crowd. As Megan had warned her, business was indeed booming over here. She wondered if that would help her own store any. It might, provided she had parking. She couldn't keep the smile from her face. She imagined Megan Phenix would be plenty mad when she found out Leah was going to install signs on each of her allotted parking spots. That would probably provoke another visit from her. She sighed. She really did need to play nice with her neighbors, she thought. Going to war over parking wasn't going to win her any friends in town. Of course, sparring with Megan Phenix had proven to be entertaining. The younger woman had just enough of a temper to be fun.

She glanced around, looking for Megan and spotting instead an older, slightly less attractive version of her. Leah smiled as she approached. Her hair was darker than Megan's and a little longer, her body more round than Megan's...but the resemblance was unmistakable. This must be the sister.

"Hi. I'm Nancy Phenix, co-owner of the grill," the woman said as she placed a frosty mug of beer down in front of her. "I understand you bought the shop next door."

Leah nodded. "Yes. I'm Leah Rollins." She held her hand out. "Pleased to meet you."

"Welcome to town, Leah," Nancy said with a big smile as she shook her hand. "I know you're still getting settled, but if you need anything, don't hesitate to ask. We're a friendly bunch here."

Leah nearly choked on her beer, wondering if these two were indeed sisters. Nancy appeared welcoming…pleasant, actually. Megan, on the other hand, was quite the opposite. In fact, Leah would go so far as to say she was a tad on the grouchy side. She had to hide a smile as she remembered Megan wadding up her note and throwing it at her before she stormed out of the bookstore. She turned her attention back to Nancy and nodded politely.

"Thank you, Nancy. I appreciate it. I'm staying at a bed-and-breakfast for a few weeks until the upstairs gets remodeled. After that, I'll be right next door."

Nancy nodded. "Yes, I heard you're staying at the Howells'." She touched Leah's arm lightly. "And don't you worry about the remodeling. Tony does excellent work."

"Well, good. Glad to hear it."

Nancy smiled again. "Well…I should get back to work. It was so nice to meet you, Leah."

"Same here. I'm sure I'll see you around."

Nancy turned to leave, then stopped, leaning close to her. "When I asked Megan how old you were, she said seventy-five," she said in a near whisper. Then she winked. "I think you look fabulous for seventy-five."

Leah was actually speechless as her gaze followed Nancy back to the bar. Was she flirting with her? And seventy-five? Well, she supposed she deserved that. Apparently Megan Phenix had a warped sense of humor. She looked around, oddly disappointed that she wasn't anywhere in sight.

* * *

Megan let out a big yawn. "I am so tired," she said. "Damn Brent and his flu."

"As if I wasn't on my feet the whole night too," Nancy said as she slid a glass of wine in her direction. "I hate bar duty."

"Standing behind the bar is not the same as waiting tables," she said.

"Well, you took a long enough break."

"Only to give you time to check out the new blood in town," she said.

Nancy smiled as she sighed wistfully. "She's so cute." Then she slapped at Megan's hand. "I can't believe you said she was seventy-five! She's probably my age."

Megan waved her hand across the bar. "Whatever. She's irritating."

"She seemed very nice."

Megan narrowed her eyes. "Do you have a crush on her or something?"

"Seeing as how I've only met her…no. But I wouldn't mind getting to know her better," Nancy said.

"She's hoarding parking spaces," Megan said. "And she's not even open for business yet!"

Nancy held up her hand. "Do not start with the parking crap again, please."

"I'm just saying…"

Nancy walked around the bar and sat down beside her, sliding the wine bottle between them. It was a familiar routine. The staff was cleaning up and Eddie had just turned the vacuum on. In the kitchen, the last of the dishes were being piled into the washers and Maria was scrubbing down the sinks. Johnny was inventorying supplies and Eileen was going over schedules for tomorrow. Ralph was going around to the windows, lowering the blinds. Another Friday in the books.

"Your roots are starting to show. And you need a haircut," Nancy said as she brushed the hair off Megan's face.

Megan nodded. "I have an appointment next week for color. Remember, I'm letting it grow, though." She glanced at her. "Do you think I should still color it? Kinda tired of blond."

"The color looks good on you," Nancy said. "You're a natural blond anyway."

"Dirty blond," Megan corrected as she tucked it behind her ears. "Barely lighter than yours."

"You could use a little trim, at least. It looks shaggy."

"Yeah…I'll see what Gloria says. She's the one who talked me into letting it grow." Megan tapped her shoulder. "Here… give me a little back rub."

Nancy let out a long sigh but stood, moving behind her. Megan moaned as her fingers squeezed her shoulders.

"You really need to get a girlfriend to do this."

"Ouch," she said as she leaned forward. "Not so damn hard."

"Again…you need a girlfriend for this."

"How can you even say that? The last one was so disastrous," she said.

"I told you she was all wrong for you. You never listen to me."

Megan rolled her eyes. "You encouraged me, if you'll recall."

"Well, at first, sure. After Tammi, I didn't think you'd ever date again."

Megan leaned her head on the bar. "Please do not bring up her name."

"Good Lord, Megan. That was over ten years ago."

"Makes no difference. She made the Wicked Witch look like a saint."

Nancy sat down beside her again. "Your problem is, you choose the wrong kind."

"What? You mean the extremely cute, charming, lying and cheating kind?"

"Well, Tammi was attractive, I'll give you that. I would never call her charming though."

"Of course she was charming," Megan said. "How else do you think she managed to cheat on me for four years?"

"Because she was conniving, not charming," Nancy said. "But you were too young to swear off dating. That's why—after eight years—I encouraged you to date Erin. My mistake. She was too cute. You can't trust women who are that pretty."

"I was perfectly happy being alone," she said. "Like now, I'm perfectly happy. Besides, we know every single woman in town and there's not a one of them I'd want to date."

Nancy sighed. "I know. We are limited here." Then she nudged Megan with her elbow. "That's why Leah Rollins intrigues me. She's new in town. And I certainly wouldn't mind dating her."

Megan rolled her eyes. "I don't know why. She's irritating as hell. In fact—"

"Oh, my God!" Eileen said as she hurried over to them. "You've got to see this." She held her phone up to them. "She's making it a contest."

"She who?" Megan asked as she stared at the phone. It was a bare ankle and foot. Her brow furrowed in a frown. That was *her* bare ankle and foot. "Are you freakin' kidding me?"

Nancy laughed. "I see Mary Beth is still having a little fun at your expense."

"Let me see that," Megan said as she jerked the phone from Eileen. "Oh. My. *God!* She's going to reveal more each day until someone guesses who the 'naked beauty' is and until that 'naked beauty' shares a romantic dinner with her." Megan glared at her sister. "She's out of her freakin' mind!"

"This is hilarious!" Eileen chimed in. "You do know that not a soul will guess your name, don't you?"

"I don't know why," Megan said. "Everyone already knows it's me." She took the phone again, flipping through Mary Beth's Facebook page. "I see she still hasn't taken that other photo down." She grimaced. "God, I look like crap."

Eileen shook her head. "You have no clue, do you?"

"What are you talking about?"

"Oh, Megan, you don't look like crap. You look like an angel, according to Mary Beth's caption, anyway," she said. "So many of the women in town have asked you out over the years and you continue to turn them all down. And now Mary Beth apparently has some compromising photos of you. You don't think they're all dying to see them?"

"Good Lord, why? I'm thirty-nine years old. And it's not like I go to the gym."

Eileen rolled her eyes. "Please," she said with a touch of disgust. "I do go to the gym and I still don't look like you." She took her phone from Megan's hand. "See you two tomorrow. Maybe Mary Beth will work her way up to your knee by then."

Nancy laughed as Megan scowled at her.

"Oh, lighten up, sis. I'm sure it's all in fun. It's been a long winter. Mary Beth is probably just trying to liven things up before tourist season."

"Glad I can be the town's amusement," she said dryly. "And I didn't turn them all down. I went out with Erin, didn't I?"

"She doesn't count. She's wasn't here long enough to be considered a local."

"Unfortunately, she didn't leave soon enough."

CHAPTER SIX

Leah sneezed as the second shelf came down and another cloud of dust drifted by. She went back to the coffee bar, trying to get out of the workers' way as they hauled the old boards out to their truck. A loud bang from upstairs made her glance to the ceiling. Was that the toilet they dropped?

"I really shouldn't be here," she murmured.

She'd stayed out of their hair for the first ten days, only coming by in the evenings when they'd left the shop. True to his word, Tony's crew was fast. She couldn't believe how quickly the bedroom walls had gone up. It gave her a better idea of how much space she'd be left with and—despite Tony's warning that it would delay the project—she'd changed the design of the kitchen. Even if it added a week to their work, she wanted the apartment the way she wanted it. It wasn't like she would be able to redo it later.

Today was the first day she'd been there while they worked. It wasn't so much she was being nosy—because she was. But her parking signs were being installed today. That thought brought a smile to her face, albeit a slightly evil smile. She hadn't seen Megan or her sister all week, but as usual, each evening when she came by, her parking spots were occupied. The parking code stipulated that she could designate five spaces in front of her shop to be exclusively hers. That was limited to business hours, of course, and she didn't yet know what her hours were going to be. Hell, she still wasn't even sure what inventory she would carry in the store.

She assumed the parking signs would be ignored since she wasn't open for business yet—as Megan had told her several times. But the mere presence of the signs would no doubt irritate Megan Phenix to no end. She didn't know why she continued to provoke her. Well, she did know why; it was fun.

Tony came down the stairs in the back, wiping his brow. He smiled when he saw her.

"Good. You're still here."

"Is there a problem?"

"No, no. But we got the bathroom all finished. Chuck is finishing up the wiring for your stove, then we'll start on the cabinets," he said. "If everything goes as planned, we'll start painting next week, then start on the flooring."

"Oh, that's great, Tony."

"So plan to have your appliances delivered, say, next week Friday."

"I can do that. Does that mean I can move in after that?"

"Well, I doubt we'll be totally finished, but my thought was to store the appliances down here and we'd move them up when we're ready. We're just getting started on the utility room."

"Okay." She tried not to sound disappointed. He'd warned her it would take four weeks, but she had been hoping to be in sooner. She was already weeks past ready to get out of the Howells' place. Not that they weren't a very sweet couple. They were—almost to a fault. Mrs. Howell had insisted she join her and her husband for dinner each evening. Maybe it was because Leah was new in town and didn't know anyone yet or maybe Mrs. Howell felt sorry for her, being homeless as she was. In order to escape dinner with them some nights, she had decided to try out some of the places in town.

There were some very nice, very expensive restaurants that she passed on. There were a handful of pubs. She assumed there were more, but she'd only noticed two Mexican food places, one advertising Tex-Mex, the other offering "authentic" food. Coming from California, she loathed Tex-Mex, and she was too suspicious of the word "authentic" to actually consider eating at that one. There was a steakhouse she'd tried; while the food was very good, the atmosphere was a bit stuffy. Another steakhouse that catered to the Harley-Davidson crowd looked inviting, but she had been too intimidated to walk in alone. There was a local pizza joint, but she passed on that. There was the Burger Barn at the edge of town and she'd tried that. But after eating at the Phenix Grill, she found the burger they served small and tasteless in comparison. And instead of crispy, spicy onion rings, she had been served limp, soggy fries.

She looked out the window, seeing the lunch crowd starting to arrive at the grill. She knew her parking spaces would be filled shortly, which made her wonder when Mr. Russell was coming by with her signs. He'd simply said "he'd swing by." She'd learned that not many in town were concerned with time and schedules, which would take her some getting used to.

Oh, well. All she could do was wait. She went back to the storage room in the back that she was going to turn into her office. Well, half of it, anyway. She'd still need a place to store her inventory...whatever that might be.

Yeah...she really needed to decide on that, didn't she? She hated to think that this whole endeavor was based on a whim, but it came close to that. Aunt Ruby had told her once that if she had to do it all over again, she'd buy a tacky little tourist shop in Idyllwild and live up in the mountains instead of Los Angeles. Leah had recalled that conversation clearly one day while sitting in an endless traffic jam. It had become a fantasy, one she could drift away to when her real life became too stressful. After Aunt Ruby died, she realized her fantasy could become a reality, if she wanted it to. Unfortunately, in all of her dreams, inventory wasn't ever covered and she wasn't certain what she wanted. T-shirts, yes. Practically every store in town sold some kind of T-shirts and most of them sold the same ones. But up here in the Ozarks, maybe she should go with wood. Like carvings or hand-made wind chimes. Maybe some chainsaw art like she'd seen on her quick trip to Branson. Maybe some cute wooden signs. Well, whatever route she decided on, it didn't mean she'd have to stick with it. She could always change. She had time. And thanks to Aunt Ruby…she had money.

* * *

"What are you doing?"

"Trying to figure out what the hell *she's* doing," Megan said as she peeked through the blinds in their office. "Gordon Russell is over there. What do you think's up with that?"

"Well, she's having remodeling done, you know," Nancy said.

Megan looked at her and shook her head. "Gordon doesn't do remodeling. Besides, Tony and his guys have been parking in the alley in the back. Gordon's truck is right out front."

"If you're so nosy, why don't you go over and ask him," she suggested.

"Her bike is there. Why don't *you* go over?"

"Because I'm not the one worried about it," Nancy said. "Although it might be a good opportunity for me to ask her out."

Megan's eyebrows shot up. "Ask her out?"

"Yes. You know…like a date."

"Are you serious?"

"I find her attractive."

"You've seen her one time," Megan pointed out.

"And? It was obviously long enough to know that she's pleasant and cute."

Megan shook her head. "I can't imagine what you see in her. She's…she's *irritating*," she said, using her favorite word to describe Leah Rollins. She peeked through the blinds again, then frowned as Gordon started up some kind of a gas-powered tool.

"What is that?" Nancy asked beside her.

"I'm not sure. Looks like he's drilling into the edge of the sidewalk."

"Whatever for?"

Megan pulled away from the blinds and stared at Nancy. "You don't think she's putting up parking signs, do you?"

Nancy shrugged. "Maybe so."

Megan put her hands on her hips. "She's not even freakin' open yet! I swear, the woman is *obsessed* with parking spaces!"

Nancy laughed. "Megan, you are the one obsessed with parking spaces."

"I'm not obsessed. I'm only concerned about our parking situation," she said. "And you should be too. Where are our customers going to park now?"

"It's only five spaces. Actually, it's only four spaces since you always hogged one of them anyway."

"You're missing the point."

"No. The point is, you're pissed that you lost your 'reserved' spot," Nancy said, making quotes in the air. "We always have more customers than our parking allows and they always park down the street and walk. Nothing has changed except you lost your prime spot. Park in the alley in the back like I do and quit taking up an extra spot up front."

Megan stared at her, slowly shaking her head. "You do remember why I have a new SUV, right?"

"It's three years old."

"Beside the point. You *do* remember why I got it, don't you?"

Nancy waved her hand in the air. "So the delivery truck smashed your car? It happened once, Megan. Once."

"It happened in the alley. And smashed doesn't exactly describe it. It looked like an accordion when he got through with it."

"You're exaggerating."

"And…and that same guy almost took out Eileen's little Honda."

"It was a scratch on her bumper."

"He is dangerous! I can't believe he still has a job." She looked back through the blinds, her eyes widening. "Oh, my God! She *is* putting up parking signs." She squinted, trying to read them. "Who the hell is Ruby?"

"Oh, for God's sake, Megan! Lighten up already. You know what your problem is?"

Megan pointed out the window. "Yeah. It's right next door."

"Your problem is, you're all uptight. You need to have sex. Wild sex. I'm sure it'll do wonders for your disposition."

Megan put her hands on her hips. "First of all, I'm not uptight. And secondly, I'm never having sex again." She paused. "Well, at least not with another person."

Nancy wrinkled up her nose. "Gross. I didn't need to hear that."

Megan rolled her eyes. "As if you haven't been single for the last ten years."

CHAPTER SEVEN

Leah knew, as a local, that she should do her grocery shopping at Susie's. Mrs. Howell had told her as much. However, as she entered the small store she wondered if it wouldn't have been advisable to go to the supermarket down the hill. Her list was long and extensive. But, if she wanted to be considered a local, she should shop like a local.

She pushed a cart in front of her as she moved slowly down the aisles. As she expected, the selection was limited. She wondered if she was going to have to make a trip out of town just to go shopping. Maybe she'd chance it and make a run to the supermarket after all and hope no one spotted her.

"Well, Leah…hello."

She turned, finding a short, plump woman with blazing red hair walking toward her. She returned Susie's smile, thinking her hair was even brighter than it had been the first time they'd met.

"Hello, Susie."

"I was wondering when I'd see you. I heard that your apartment was finished and that they'd moved your appliances in this morning."

Leah didn't bother asking how she knew this already. Mrs. Howell had warned her that Susie was the town's gossip.

"Yes, Tony got it all finished. He did a great job."

"Well, I'm sure you're anxious to get moved in. He starts work on Monday, right? For the downstairs?"

She nodded. "They've already taken down most of the shelves. He said two weeks at the most," she said. "By the way, I'm looking for organic olive oil. A California brand, if you have it."

Susie laughed. "Oh, honey, olive oil is olive oil." She reached for a bottle and placed it in Leah's cart. "Now, have you met very many people in town? I know you've met Nancy and Megan, of course. They're just the sweetest, aren't they?"

Leah scratched the back of her neck absently, hiding a smile. "Oh, they certainly are. Nancy especially," she added.

"Nancy is close to your age, I guess. I'm sure you would have more in common with her." She waved her hand. "Megan is still a young thing," she said with a laugh. "Although she has issues," she said, lowering her voice.

Leah's interest was piqued. "Oh?"

"Women issues," she whispered. "In that she has the worst luck."

"I see."

Susie shook her head. "Oh, but I don't like to gossip. It's not really my business." She looked around, seeing no one listening to them, then she leaned closer. "The poor thing was heartbroken when they moved here. Took her eight years before she'd date anyone. And then, she chooses Erin Wright, of all people. She wasn't even a local," Susie said, waving her hand in the air. "Her father bought the old Stafford House and turned it into a B&B. She was in town long enough to make Megan fall in love with her, then she promptly cheated on her with a seasonal worker, of all things. Megan found out about it on her birthday and was heartbroken all over again. Thank God Erin and her new flame moved out of town. Why, it was downright awkward around here for a while."

"I'm sure it was," Leah said.

"Well, that was a year ago. Now it looks like Mary Beth is making a play for her." Susie laughed. "And don't believe what you see on Facebook. As I hear it, it was only in Mary Beth's dreams that they slept together the night of her birthday." Then her smile faltered a little. "Of course, she is in possession of Megan's red bra." She shook her head quickly. "No, no. I'm sure she stole it."

Leah stared at her, not sure what kind of reply that statement warranted. "Well, I'm not friends on Facebook with anyone here yet so I'm out of the loop, I'm afraid."

"Oh, honey, we can't have that," Susie said with a laugh. "How do you expect to keep up? Do you have your phone? You can friend me right now and I'll hook you up with everyone."

In the blink of an eye, Leah found herself "hooked up" with half the town. Thankfully, someone needed Susie's attention and she was left in peace. But as she browsed through the produce section, her curiosity got the better of her. As discreetly as she could, she pulled up Mary Beth Sturgeon's page.

"Wow," she murmured as her eyes were glued to a bare thigh. A bare thigh, firm calf and very nice foot. She flipped through more pictures, each one less revealing than the thigh. She finally found one of Megan in bed, obviously asleep, lying on her stomach, the sheet reaching only up as far as her lower back. "God, she's cute," she whispered. Then she frowned. What would Megan Phenix possibly see in Mary Beth Sturgeon?

She heard voices behind her and she quickly pocketed her phone, embarrassed for nearly having been caught looking. But as Susie had said, how was she going to keep up with everything if not through Facebook?

* * *

Megan literally groaned when she saw Mary Beth step into the grill. She narrowed her eyes at her.

"What are you doing here?"

Mary Beth gave her a big smile. "Oh, angel, I came to see you, of course."

Megan's mouth dropped open as Mary Beth pulled her shirt off her shoulder slightly, revealing the strap of a red bra. *Her* bra!

"*Jesus*," she hissed. "Cover that up before someone sees you!"

"Can we talk?" Mary Beth asked. "Alone?"

"I don't think that's a good idea," she said. "I'm likely to strangle you."

Mary Beth laughed. "Oh, you're so funny, Megan. But I have a proposition."

"Whatever it is…no."

"No?" Again, a syrupy smile. "Have you seen my Facebook page today?" Then she laughed. "No, of course you haven't. I forgot. I had to block you. We're up above your knee."

Megan gritted her teeth, counting to ten. Well, she made it to five, at least. "What…do…you…want?"

"A date."

"A date? Well, to hear everyone in town talk, we've already had a date. I mean, you *are* wearing my bra."

"Craig will reserve a table for us. Prime rib. Wine. Candlelight." She batted her eyes. "Very romantic."

Megan took her arm and pulled her to the side, away from curious stares. "Look, I know you're having a little fun here with my picture on Facebook and all…but really, why would you want to go on a date with me?"

"Everyone wants to go on a date with you. You play hard to get."

"I don't play hard to get," she insisted, shocked that Mary Beth would even think so. "There's no one in town I want to date! That's not playing hard to get!"

"I know, I know…you swore off women. We all know the story, Megan," Mary Beth said. "But obviously you didn't swear off them *totally*. I mean, Erin waltzed into town and swept you off your feet."

Megan rolled her eyes. "I wouldn't exactly call it sweeping me off my feet," she murmured.

"And then she dumps you and leaves you here with a broken heart…and now you've again sworn off women. Well, we can't be that choosy, Megan. You know, the town isn't that big."

"Tell me about it," she muttered.

Mary Beth shook her head. "Younger women," she said disgustedly. "You should know better, Megan. You can't trust them. Me? I'm fifty-three. I'm mature. I'm—"

"Mature? *Really?* You have my freakin' photo on Facebook and you're *wearing my bra!*"

"And it's a very nice bra too," she said. "Now…how long will you hold out before you go out with me?"

"I'm not going out with you! I'm not *ever* going out with you."

Mary Beth's smile never faltered. "You know, there's not a whole lot left after the thigh. Another leg…arms…stomach… all before we get to the good part."

God…are you freakin' kidding me?

"You know what…Nancy is forty-seven. Much closer to your age. And you know…she's looking to date. Unlike me. I'm not ever dating again. But Nancy…she's on the market, if you get my drift."

"Oh, Megan, really? Nancy and I are friends. I wouldn't want to date her." She looked past Megan and waved. "But I should at least go over and say hello to her." She patted Megan's arm, letting her hand linger there. "I'll see you before too long."

CHAPTER EIGHT

"Do you think I should get a restraining order?"

Nancy looked at her and frowned. "For Mary Beth?"

"Yes, for Mary Beth," she snapped.

"Get serious. Mary Beth is harmless."

"Harmless? She's a stalker!" She pointed to the laptop. "Bring up her Facebook page. I want to see how far she's gone."

"Your upper thigh. I will say, it's quite an alluring shot. I had no idea your legs were that nice."

Megan groaned and covered her face. "This has got to stop. I'm starting to get whistled at in town." She pulled her hands away. "She is going to stop, right? I mean, tourist season officially starts on Friday. So she's going to stop, right?"

"I imagine so. I told you, she's just having a little fun." Nancy laughed. "You can't go anywhere in town without someone talking about it. And the fact that she had to block you on Facebook is hilarious."

"Oh, right…it's freakin' *hysterical*," Megan said sarcastically.

"Well, you could put an end to it," Nancy said. "Simply go out with her. That's all she wants."

Megan went to the window and looked out, seeing their neighbor's bicycle propped up against the storefront. She turned back to Nancy. "First of all, I can't believe you'd even suggest that," she said. "And if I thought that would put an end to it, I might just do it. But it would set a precedent," she said with a wave of her hand. "Then Julie would ask me out. And Melissa. And then Sarah."

"True. Sarah was all over you at your birthday party."

"She was?" She shook her head. "That night is still a blur."

"Speaking of parties, Susie told me that the kickoff party will be at Craig's on Thursday."

"I thought it was Paul and Michael's turn," she said.

"They're having some last-minute painting done or something," Nancy said. "Anyway, I'm getting Johnny to whip up a big batch of queso. You're in charge of the chips."

"Thank you. I can handle that." She looked out the window again. "Do you think the crazy lady next door got invited?"

"Oh, I'm sure. Susie said she visited with her the other day. Seems she's super nice. Susie said she hooked her up with everybody on Facebook so she'll be in the loop."

Megan's eyes widened. "Oh, my God. *Facebook?*"

"Oh...yeah," Nancy said with a smile. "You're kinda all out there, aren't you?"

The ringing of Megan's phone kept her from issuing a snarky retort. She looked at her phone, then looked at Nancy.

"It's Mom."

"So answer it."

"She always calls you, not me." She raised her eyebrows. "You think something's wrong?"

"Answer the phone already. I'm going to the kitchen to help prep," Nancy said.

She took a deep breath. "Hi Mom," she greeted cheerfully. Then her smile faded. "What's wrong?"

"Wrong? What makes you think something is wrong," her mother said. "Can't I call and see how you are?"

"Mom…you talk to Nancy twice a week."

"Well, I talk to Nancy. I don't talk to *you*." She cleared her throat. "So…how are things?"

"As if she hasn't already told you what's going on," she said as she sat down at the desk.

"I don't know what you're talking about."

"So you don't know about the Facebook page?"

"What Facebook page?"

"You don't know that I'm being blackmailed on Facebook?"

"Oh, my God! That's terrible."

Megan rolled her eyes. "Oh, give me a break! You can't even fake it!"

Her mother laughed heartily. "Well, Nancy says it's a really good picture. I understand she's up to your thigh."

"Yeah, she's up to my thigh. If she goes any higher, I'll have to shoot her. I hope you and Dad will visit me in prison."

Her mother laughed again. "I take it you have no intention of going out with her."

"Absolutely not," she said.

"Okay. So what's up with the woman who bought the bookstore? Nancy says she's really nice."

"Nice?"

"And cute. Is there something going on there?"

"As far as I know, she's only seen her the one time here at the grill," she said. "Besides, I can't imagine what Nancy would see in her. She's annoying. Irritating."

"Nancy said she was very pleasant."

"Pleasant? She's infuriating. Did she tell you about the parking?"

"No."

"No, of course she'd leave *that* part out—the main thing that's going on." She got up and went to the window, looking out at the bookstore. "She's hoarding parking spaces. She's not even freakin' open yet and she puts up these signs." She stared at the offending signs. "Ruby's Parking Only. Who the hell is Ruby?"

"Well, it sounds like you had a run-in with her."

"A run-in? She's evil. I think she enjoyed tossing me out of my reserved spot. A bully. A *mean* bully," she said.

"That's odd. Nancy had a completely different impression of her than you do."

"That's because she obviously put on an act with Nancy. Underneath it all...she's the spawn of Satan."

Her mother laughed. "Oh, Megan, we should talk more often. You always make me laugh."

"Well, happy to provide some amusement for you," she said dryly. "Are you and Dad still planning to come visit in June?" she asked, changing the subject.

"Yes, but it might be early June instead of late. Your dad has this crazy idea to drive all the way to Niagara Falls. We're still debating that plan," she said. "Well, I should run. Love you, Megan."

"Love you too," she said, barely getting the words out before her mother ended the call.

She sighed, then glanced once more out the window, watching as Leah Rollins hopped on her bike and rode off down the street.

CHAPTER NINE

As Leah stood in the doorway of the Ozark Room, the large event room at Craig's restaurant, she wished she'd gone with her first inclination—stay home and get her apartment in order. But if she was going to fit in around here, she needed to get out and meet everyone. However, there was not a single familiar face in the room. She didn't even spot Susie with her blazing red hair.

There was a short, round woman with bleached hair, spiked on top. A man with a bowl cut hairdo stood next to her. Oops. No, it was a woman. Behind them were two men in matching suspenders—red—talking to a tall woman with long dark hair, wearing a tie-dyed dress.

"They're a scary bunch. Afraid to go in?"

The familiar voice brought a smile to her face and she turned, surprised that she'd consider Megan Phenix—of all people— a "friendly face" in this crowd of strangers.

"A bit out of my element," she admitted. "I don't recognize a soul. Perhaps I came too early."

Megan turned, pulling her sister Nancy up beside her. "You remember Nancy, don't you? Now you recognize someone."

A quick smile and Megan was gone, leaving her standing face-to-face with her older sister. She smiled politely at her.

"Good to see you again, Nancy."

Nancy's hand wrapped around her forearm casually. "I'm glad you came. Susie said she thought you'd be here."

"I decided it was time I met everyone," Leah said.

"Yes, most everyone comes to the kickoff party but not all. Diversity weekend, finally. It's exciting, isn't it?"

Leah nodded. "Although I'm not sure exactly what that entails," she said.

"The official start of tourist season," Nancy explained. "There are three diversity weekends each year. April, August and November. The town will be crawling with gays and lesbians. Get some rainbow flags to put outside your shop. The whole town turns into one giant rainbow on those weekends," Nancy said with a laugh.

"Well, I'll definitely be open for business by August so I'll keep that in mind."

Nancy drew her into the room. "Are you moved into your apartment yet? I hadn't heard."

After spending most of her life in cities, this small town gossip was going to take a while to get used to, Leah realized. Apparently there were no secrets in this town.

"It's getting there," she said. "My new furniture was delivered, so I have my bedroom set up, that's the main thing. When I came to town, I didn't bring much with me, but I'm in the process of sorting through it." She shrugged. "A trip to California is in the plans," she said. "I hope to be able to bring the rest of my things over in one trip."

"Where in California?"

"San Jose," she said.

"That'll be quite a road trip." Nancy waved at the two men in suspenders. "You've got to meet George and Peter," she said. "They're a hoot. They own the candle shop down on the corner of Cliff Street. They make all their own stuff."

And so it went, little by little, Nancy dragging her around the room, introducing her to more and more people. She'd long lost track of their names, but she was pleased to see Tony there, although she hardly recognized him without his ball cap and work clothes. His partner, Steve, was much older than he was but very friendly. After visiting with him, she almost wished she'd taken Tony up on his offer to rent one of Steve's cottages. It would have been a lot less stressful than spending nearly six weeks with the Howells.

She looked around the room, finding Megan talking to an attractive woman with jet-black hair. Nancy followed her gaze.

"Oh, that's Carla," Nancy said. "She owns the art gallery down the street from us." Nancy leaned closer. "She's been asking Megan out for years. Watch…Megan will hold her hands up and start backing up." Nancy laughed as Megan did just that. "She's making up some excuse as to why she can't go out with her."

"Well, I'm not one to gossip, but Susie said that Mary Beth was interested in her." Then she laughed quietly. "Although if that's so, exposing her on Facebook might not be the best plan."

"Have you met Mary Beth?"

Leah shook her head. "Not yet."

"She fancies herself as a bit of a player," Nancy explained. "And in her younger days, she was. But she's older now and… well, Megan's just not interested." She smiled. "Not even a little."

"If you don't mind my asking, how does Mary Beth have these pictures of her? Susie hinted that while it may look like they slept together, they really didn't."

Nancy laughed. "Oh, that's a story for another day. Why don't you come by the grill for lunch next week and we'll chat." Once again her hand reached out to touch Leah's arm. "I would love to get to know you better."

Of the two Phenix sisters, Nancy was definitely the pleasant one. And Leah certainly wouldn't mind making a new friend. However, judging by the look in Nancy's eyes, she had something a little more intimate in mind. Leah chose to ignore the subtle hint.

"I might take you up on the lunch offer," she said easily. "Really, the only reason I came to the party tonight was to meet more of the shop owners in town. I hope they're all as friendly as you are."

"We're a diverse group, that's for sure," Nancy said. "For the most part, everyone gets along fine. Tourist season is busy and hectic and we don't have much leisure time then. We'll have another one of these parties after Labor Day, when things start slowing down again."

"Susie told me that the town didn't really slow down until after the Christmas holidays."

"People come for the fall colors in late October, but it's not as busy as summer. November is pretty quiet, but most of the B&Bs are booked between Thanksgiving and New Year's," Nancy said. "After that, we pretty much get the town back to ourselves for a few months." She looked past her and shook her head. "I should probably go rescue Megan. Julie's got her now." Nancy smiled at her. "Come with me. I'll introduce you."

Leah followed her gaze, seeing a rail-thin woman with light brown hair talking to Megan. Megan appeared to be trying to back away from her, but the woman's mouth never stopped moving and her hand was resting lightly on Megan's arm. The look on Megan's face nearly made Leah laugh. It was a mixture of terror and exasperation, and when she and Nancy walked over, the relief on her face was visible.

"Julie, have you met Leah Rollins?" Megan asked quickly. "She bought the old bookstore next to us."

Julie turned her attention toward her, and Leah could see the predatory look in her eyes. Julie took a step closer to Megan, as if defending her territory.

"We've not met," Julie said, her voice as thin as she was. "I've heard about you, of course."

Leah smiled and nodded. Of course.

"Julie owns Cliff Street Chocolates," Nancy supplied. "And on hot summer days, her ice cream sundaes are not to be missed."

"I'm not much for chocolate," Leah admitted, "but I do have a weakness for ice cream."

"Well, you'll need to come by sometime," Julie said.

Megan took that opportunity to take a step away from Julie. "You'll have to excuse us, Julie," Megan said. "I have some… some business to speak to Leah about."

Leah's eyebrows shot up.

"What kind of business?" Julie asked.

"It involves…parking," Megan said.

Nancy laughed. "It could get ugly," she said, taking Julie's arm and leading her away, giving Megan a quick wink.

As soon as they were out of earshot, Megan groaned. "God, she wears me out."

"I take it she's enamored with your glowing personality?" Leah asked.

Megan's eyes narrowed. "Really?"

Leah smiled. "Teasing, of course."

Megan put her hands on her hips. "Speaking of parking… *really*? *Signs*?"

Leah shrugged. "Gordon assured me that there were many businesses in town that put up parking signs," she said.

"I wouldn't say 'many,'" Megan said. "But those that do are at least open for business."

"I want to be prepared for when I do open," Leah said, trying desperately to keep the smile from her face. She didn't know why, but annoying Megan Phenix had become a favorite pastime. "Besides, I think you're only pissed because you lost your prime spot. From what I see, your customers park down the street anyway."

"Again, you're missing the point entirely," Megan said.

Leah shrugged again. "Why don't you just park in the back?"

Megan shook her head. "I don't park in the back."

"Why? Afraid you'll get mugged in the alley or something?"

"Funny," Megan said dryly. "No. I'm afraid of Max."

Leah frowned. Was Max some dog running wild that she needed to be aware of? "Who is Max?"

"Max is the delivery guy."

Leah shook her head. "Okay. You lost me. Max is dangerous?"

"Yes, Max is dangerous," Megan said, as if Leah should have already known that. "Max has spatial awareness problems."

"Oh. I see," she said, not really understanding.

"He runs into things," Megan explained. "With his truck."

"Ah. Gotcha."

Megan looked past her, her eyes widening. "Oh, *God*," she groaned.

Leah turned, following her gaze.

"It's Mary Beth Sturgeon," Megan murmured, nearly jerking Leah in front of her to shield her.

Leah had to contain a giggle. So this was the infamous Mary Beth? She was older than Leah would have thought from looking at her Facebook photo, which obviously was dated. She was a few pounds overweight, but she wouldn't call her fat. The way she carried herself, yes, she could imagine her being a "player" in her younger days, as Nancy had suggested. And while she didn't pretend to know Megan Phenix in the least, there was no way she could picture the two of them together.

"So she's the one posting your photo on Facebook, huh?"

Megan groaned again. "I suppose you've seen it?"

"From what I've gathered, I think the whole town has seen it," she said with a laugh.

As Mary Beth walked across the room, Megan continued to hide behind Leah, moving slightly as Leah did. Mary Beth finally disappeared into the crowd.

"I think it's safe now," she said.

"She's insane," Megan muttered.

"So how did she get your picture?" Leah asked. "Or was that a private moment between the two of you?"

Megan's eyes widened. "No! I did not *sleep* with her," she hissed. She blew out her breath. "It was my birthday. I drank too much Patrón." Her voice lowered conspiratorially. "I personally think someone drugged me. Like Mary Beth."

"Oh?"

Megan sighed. "The party was at her house. My no-good sister thought it would be a good idea to leave me there." Megan waved her hand in the air dismissively. "I woke up the next morning—naked—in her bed. And *she* was naked. I freaked out."

"I don't blame you." Then she lowered her voice. "Are you sure you didn't sleep with her?"

Megan punched her in the arm. "Don't even think that, much less say it out loud."

Leah couldn't contain her laughter as she rubbed her arm. "I suppose if you had, she wouldn't be doing the whole Facebook thing, huh? What does she hope to accomplish?"

"She wants me to go out with her...a romantic dinner," Megan said. "I guess she thinks if I go out with her, I'll see her in a new light and fall in love or something." Megan gave an exaggerated shudder. "As if."

"Wouldn't it be easier to simply go out with her one time and end this?"

"That's just it. It wouldn't end. If I go out with Mary Beth, then Julie will insist I go out with her. Then Sarah. Then Melissa. Then Carla. It would never end."

"Wow. Must be nice to be so popular," she said.

"Popular has nothing to do with it," Megan said. "I'm the youngest single woman in town. And...well...they think I'm playing hard to get. It's some contest between them." Then Megan's eyes narrowed. "Why am I telling you all this?"

Leah shrugged. "I'm easy to talk to."

"I don't even like you," Megan said as she took a step away from her. "But thank you for hiding me from Mary Beth."

And with that, Megan Phenix hurried away. Leah watched her for a second, smiling as Megan hugged an older gentleman, pausing to kiss him on the cheek before walking on.

CHAPTER TEN

"Everything is so bubbly! I love it when the gays come to town," Nancy said as she filled a mug with draft beer.

"You must," Megan said. "You flood the place with enough rainbow flags."

"Diversity weekend...of course we're flooding the grill with flags."

Megan moved one aside that was hanging in her face. "I need a vodka tonic with lemon instead of lime and a gin fizz."

"I hate gin fizz," Nancy said. "Who drinks those things?"

"One of your gays," she said with a laugh.

"Got to be a guy. No lesbian would order it."

Megan got bumped from behind. "We're packed tonight. I don't remember it being this busy last year."

"The more the merrier," Nancy said. "One of these days, a rich old woman is going to come in here and steal me away."

Megan rolled her eyes. Nancy said the same thing every year. "I thought you had your sights set on the crazy woman next door."

"I wish. She's so cute. And I did get to visit with her a couple of times at the party last night, but I don't think I'm her type."

"You don't even know her."

"She rides her bike around town and drives an electric car. You and I both drive SUVs."

"So? They're practical up here. She'll learn that come wintertime. If she lasts that long," she added.

"Yeah…but the bike. I haven't been on a bike since I was a teenager. At least you jog."

Megan shook her head. "I run on a treadmill. That's not jogging. I'd die if I jogged around town with all these hills."

Nancy slid over the gin fizz, then went about making the vodka tonic. "I should take it up. I mean, look what it's done to your legs. It's all anyone in town is talking about."

"Can we not get through even one day without talking about the damn Facebook page?"

Nancy laughed. "I heard from a very good source that next week's picture will be rather revealing."

Megan took the two drinks off the bar. "You know, it disturbs me that you find this as humorous as you do."

* * *

Leah stood at the window in her living room, looking down at the Phenix Grill. Cars lined the street in both directions, and yes, all of the spots in front of her shop were taken. Of course, it was eight p.m. When she did finally open for business, she would most likely close at five or six, like most of the other shops in town.

She turned away from the window and went back to her unpacking. She had only brought the bare minimum with her, choosing to purchase new furniture instead of hauling hers cross-country. But most of her things, the things she wanted to keep, were in storage in San Jose. She realized just how little she'd brought with her when her last box was emptied and her kitchen cabinets and drawers remained mostly bare. Perhaps it was time to plan her return trip to pick up the rest of her things.

She broke down the last empty box and took it downstairs where the others were stacked by the front door. Carl had said he would take them off for her on Monday when his crew returned. She left the lights off downstairs as she glanced again toward the grill. Laughter and music could be heard each time the door opened, but it wasn't overly loud. Thankfully, the outdoor patio was on the opposite side of the building. She'd been warned by the real estate agent—when she'd mentioned having her apartment upstairs—that they often had live music on the patio during the summer months. At the time, she hadn't thought it would bother her. She was normally glued to her computer and rarely went to bed before midnight.

But now, as she watched smiling and laughing people coming and going from the grill, she felt a twinge of loneliness. Since she'd quit her job, her computer was no longer the friend that it had been. In fact, she found she loathed it. She used her phone or her iPad, leaving her laptop to sit idle.

She sighed, not knowing why she would feel lonely. She was used to spending most of her evenings alone. The dates she'd gone out on had been few and far between. The lively atmosphere next door, though, reminded her of the Friday happy hours with work friends and she had an urge to join in on the fun. Of course, she'd already had dinner, if you could call it that. The frozen burrito that she'd heated in the microwave had looked better than it tasted. Even the last of the bottle of zinfandel hadn't helped.

That was another reason she should head back to California sooner rather than later. She had one bottle of wine remaining and judging by the very limited selection of California reds in the local liquor store, she'd be drinking French wine before too long. Which, of course, would be blasphemy. Or perhaps she could talk the owner into ordering wine specifically for her.

She sighed again and finally turned from the window and made her way back upstairs. She went about closing the blinds, then settled down on her new sofa and picked up the remote. Before long, thoughts of loneliness—and her dwindling wine supply—faded as she found herself absorbed in a movie, albeit one she'd seen twice before. She never could resist Sandra Bullock.

CHAPTER ELEVEN

Leah sat at the bar nibbling on spicy onion rings as Nancy filled a mug with beer.

"Going on eleven years," Nancy said in response to Leah's question. "Hard to believe we've been here that long."

"Why here?" she asked.

Nancy placed the mug of beer in front of her, despite Leah's assertion that it was too early in the day for a drink. The spiciness of the onion rings made her reach for it anyway.

"Megan had just ended a relationship and she wanted to get away. I was managing a diner, barely making enough to pay my bills." Nancy laughed. "So yeah, we both quit our jobs. Crazy, I know."

"Did Megan also work in the restaurant business?"

"No, no. She worked at a bank. She was a loan officer. That came in pretty handy when we started this."

"It seems you've made a success though," she said, glancing around at the lunch crowd.

"The first year was scary," Nancy said. "We weren't even breaking even most months and if our parents hadn't helped us out, we'd have folded." She shrugged. "But we stuck it out through the lean months and here we are," she said with smile.

"So this all started because Megan ended a relationship, huh?" she asked, hoping she didn't sound as curious as she really was.

"Oh, it was awful," Nancy said, then she looked around them in all directions. "And she'd kill me if she knew I was telling you this," she said, her voice lowered.

"I don't gossip, if that's what you're worrying about."

Nancy laughed. "Oh, everyone already knows. Megan just doesn't like to talk about it. In fact, she doesn't even like to think about it."

"The woman was cheating on her, I suppose?"

"God, yes. The whole time they were together. We all knew it."

"Why didn't you tell her?"

"Oh, I tried, but Megan wouldn't believe me. It wasn't until she actually caught her that she realized that everyone had been telling her the truth." Nancy grimaced. "And it got ugly. I have never seen Megan so mad before." She lowered her voice again. "She took all of Tammi's stuff and threw it out on the front lawn and set fire to it."

Leah nearly laughed, but Nancy's expression was serious. She wiped the smile from her face, waiting for Nancy to continue.

"Tammi called the police. It went downhill from there."

Leah's eyes widened. "Did she get arrested?"

"No, thankfully. It was her house, not Tammi's. But what with the fire department getting called to the scene and the police showing up, it made the paper. The neighbors all thought they were living next door to a psychopath and refused to let their children out on the street." Leah's voice turned to a whisper. "It was Halloween."

At that, Leah did laugh as she pictured Megan, dressed in a witch costume or something, frantically tossing her lover's possessions into a fire as the neighbors looked on in fright.

"Sorry, but it's a vivid picture," she said around her laughter.

Nancy laughed quietly too. "We don't talk about it—ever. But it was hysterical. I hated Tammi." Then her smile faded. "Of course, after that, Megan wouldn't trust anyone." She shook her head. "Took eight years before she'd date again. Eight! I still can't believe she went out with Erin. I never liked her from the moment I saw her."

"Erin?" she asked, not wanting Nancy to know that Susie had already told her this story.

Nancy waved her question away. "Oh, that's a long story too. Erin was much younger. Too pretty for her own good. They dated for about six months. Then on Megan's birthday last year, Erin broke up with her. She'd been seeing someone else all along."

"Ouch."

"Big time. But Erin wasn't a local. Thankfully, she moved away."

"Huh. Wonder what's wrong with her?"

Nancy frowned. "What do you mean?"

Leah shrugged. "Well, two women have cheated on her. Must be something wrong with her."

"There's nothing wrong with her," Nancy insisted. "In fact, the problem is, she's too trusting." She threw her hands up. "And God, she falls for the wrong kind of women. I mean, everyone could see that Erin wasn't going to be faithful. She flirted with everybody in town. And before that, God, Tammi had a reputation a mile long, yet Megan trusted her."

Leah nodded. "So just bad luck then, huh."

"The worst."

"And now Mary Beth has pictures. This is the most recent birthday?"

Nancy nodded. "Partially my fault, partially too much tequila."

"Oh? Mary Beth doesn't get any blame?"

"It's harmless fun."

Leah shrugged. "If it was happening to me, I'm not sure how harmless I would think it was." She shrugged, smiled briefly and picked up another onion ring. "How far do you think she'll go?"

"Who knows? I wouldn't put anything past Mary Beth. I guess I am going to have to talk to her at some point." Nancy leaned closer. "Please don't let Megan know I told you all this. She'd kill me." Then she smiled. "Or set fire to me."

Leah smiled too. "Megan doesn't really like me and I kinda find her annoying. I doubt we'll have the opportunity to chat any time soon," she said as she finished the beer. "Besides, I'm leaving in the morning. Flying back to San Jose."

"Oh, really? How long will you be gone?"

"I'll only be there a day. I've rented a van so I'll drive that back here with the rest of my things. I hope to be back by Friday."

* * *

Megan was shocked to find Leah Rollins sitting at the bar chatting with Nancy. The large platter of onion rings and the empty beer mug suggested she'd come for lunch. She ducked into the hallway past the kitchen, then peeked back out. Neither Nancy nor Leah had seen her, it seemed. She took that opportunity to observe Leah Rollins freely. She admitted she was attractive. And while she wasn't really a fan of gray hair, it looked stunning on Leah. Shorter over the ears, just enough to partially cover them…longer in the back, not quite reaching the collar of her blouse. Parted on the side and swept across her forehead, the bangs barely touched her eyebrows. Dark eyebrows, she noted, not gray like her hair.

"What are you doing?"

Startled, Megan jumped and let out a tiny scream before she could cover her mouth. She turned, glaring at Eileen.

"Must you sneak up on me?"

"You look like you're up to no good."

"I was…heading to the office," she said lamely. "Excuse me."

Of course, to get to the office meant she'd have to pass by the bar. How rude would it be to ignore Nancy and Leah? She shrugged. She didn't really care.

So she walked briskly past the bar, never once glancing in their direction although the sound of Leah's quiet laughter annoyed her for some reason.

CHAPTER TWELVE

Megan drove slowly past the grill, not finding a single parking space available. She hit the steering wheel lightly. Of course. It was Friday. They opened at ten on Fridays and she was always amazed that some people would come that early for lunch. She glanced at the clock on her dash—ten forty-three. Nancy would kill her. It was her turn to tend bar.

"People don't need to be drinking this early," she murmured. Then her eyes narrowed as she saw a familiar figure walking toward the grill.

Mary Beth Sturgeon.

"Oh, crap."

She pulled into the first available parking spot and ducked down, then slithered across the console and into the passenger's seat. She peeked above the dash. Good...Mary Beth hadn't seen her. She opened the passenger's door as quietly as possible, then got out, ducking down along the side of her SUV. She went to the edge and raised her head, seeing Mary Beth on the sidewalk in front of the grill, glancing around. She ducked back down quickly, praying Mary Beth hadn't spied her yet.

"What in the world are you doing?"

Megan jumped, hitting her head on the side mirror in the process. "Shit," she muttered as she rubbed her head. She turned, seeing Leah Rollins standing in front of her shop. Megan ducked down again and held a finger to her lips. "Shhh."

"You're in a reserved parking spot for Ruby's."

"Oh, for the love," she said as she rolled her eyes, choosing to ignore the teasing tone of Leah's words. She motioned behind her toward the grill. Leah followed her gaze, a quick smile forming, followed by a short laugh.

"Oh, I see. Well, if you want to hide, come on inside."

Megan silently groaned. What? Were they actually going to be friendly with each other? No. Leah was a psycho crazy woman obsessed with parking spaces, she reminded herself. But it beat an encounter with Mary Beth Spurgeon.

She crouched down and duck-walked across the sidewalk and into Leah's shop. She let out a relieved breath as Leah closed the door behind her.

"Thank you."

"Well, if you're going to park in one of my spots, you should at least come inside," Leah said.

Megan put her hands on her hips. "Who the hell is Ruby?"

Leah laughed. "My great-aunt. She's the reason I was able to buy this place."

"Oh. Well, remind me to send her a thank-you note," Megan said sarcastically, causing Leah to laugh again.

"She's dead. Inheritance."

"Oh. Sorry."

Leah waved her apology away. "It's been nearly a year now."

Megan looked around, noticing the difference in the shop. "You've been busy," she said.

"Tony's been busy," Leah corrected.

"Mr. Carlton didn't do much to the place when he owned it, other than put in the coffee bar," she said.

"I thought he was the one who put in the reading room upstairs," Leah said.

Megan shook her head. "No. That was already there when he bought the place, books and all." She paused. "You know, he was kind enough to let me park out front there," she said, pointing.

"Yes, I gathered that," Leah said. "Perhaps that's why his business failed—he didn't have enough parking spaces for his customers."

"Ha ha," Megan said.

Leah smiled. "You want to take a look around?" she offered. "My apartment is finished, if you ignore the boxes I brought back from San Jose. I haven't gotten everything unpacked yet."

Megan frowned. "Have you been gone?"

"Oh, I see you didn't miss me, huh?" Again, an easy smile as she headed up the stairs. "I made a quick trip to California last week for the rest of my things."

Megan glanced out of the window, wondering if it was safe to go back out or not. She really had no desire to be on friendly terms with Leah Rollins. However, she was just curious enough to want to take a peek inside her apartment.

"How did you get everything back here?" she asked as she followed her up.

"I flew out, then rented a van to drive back."

Megan gave a mock gasp. "Surely not a gas-guzzling van, Leah? That's horrible!"

Leah laughed loudly but said nothing as she opened the door at the top of the stairs. Megan had only been up there a couple of times when Mr. Carlton owned the bookstore. It had been a dark room, lit by lamps only. The transformation was amazing.

"Wow," she said. "This looks great." She walked immediately to the wall of windows that looked down on Spring Street, then realizing she was in anyone's line of sight, she jumped back.

"It's okay," Leah said. "They're tinted. You can't see in during the day. Or so Tony says. I haven't actually tested it."

Megan didn't want to take a chance, so she turned away, glancing around instead. The kitchen was spacious with a large island and bar separating it from the living room. The open concept was very inviting even with boxes piled on the countertops.

Leah walked past the kitchen and opened a door. "Utility room in here. It's kinda small but manageable." Another door opened into a half-bath. "My bedroom and bath are back there," Leah said, walking opposite the kitchen. "I wasn't sure about traffic noise so I thought it best to be in the back instead of the front."

She opened that door as well and Megan peeked in, finding an exceptionally neat and tidy room. The windows opened up to the alley in the back, but large oak trees shielded the view.

"Nice. I love the design," she said honestly. "All I remember this being was a dark, drab room."

"Yes. Downstairs as well," Leah said. "You probably didn't notice, but Tony put in three additional windows in the front."

Megan nodded. "I thought it looked different," she said.

They went back into the living room, and Leah motioned to the kitchen. "Can I offer you something to drink? I know it looks a mess, but it's mostly stocked."

Megan knew she should be leaving already. Nancy was going to be pissed that she was late. But the prospect of running into Mary Beth sealed it.

"I'll have a water, if you have it."

Leah went into the kitchen and Megan leaned on the bar, looking around. She arched an eyebrow as she spied three boxes of wine. Leah laughed as she followed her gaze.

"I'm afraid I'm a snobbish Californian," she said. "I stocked up on my favorites."

"I like a good merlot," Megan said. "Although I doubt I could tell the difference between California wine and, say, French."

"Vast difference," Leah said, then smiled. "But I'm biased. That's probably the one thing I'll miss most about California—doing the wine tour a couple of times a year."

Megan sat down on a barstool as Leah stayed on the other side of the island, leaning casually against it.

"What made you come here?" she asked.

Leah shrugged. "I had my fill of big cities. I worked in the tech industry since college and I'd had my fill of computers too," she said. "When Aunt Ruby died, I suddenly had the opportunity to do something different."

"And you picked tiny Eureka Springs?"

"I wanted something small, yet gay-friendly. I mean, I'm from California. I didn't want to end up somewhere where I'd have to be in the closet to own a business," she said. "I was shocked to find this place. Two thousand full-time residents and almost half of them gay? It was too good to be true."

Megan laughed. "Well, probably not quite half, but we have a large percentage, that's for sure."

"Everyone's been pretty nice...helpful," Leah said. "I'm not used to such small towns where everyone has a connection with someone. If I need something, I ask Tony. If he can't do it, he tells me who can." She smiled. "Like Gordon and the parking signs."

"Yeah...good ole Gordon," she said dryly.

Leah laughed good-naturedly. "So I met Julie. And of course, Mary Beth. And I also met someone named Melissa. I can't see you dating any of them."

"I know, right? But they apparently *can* see it," Megan said. "What about you? Have they asked you out yet?"

Leah nodded. "A woman named Kathy that I met at the party. And Melissa. I made an excuse for both. I'm not interested in that at all."

"It's just a matter of time before they all hit you up, my sister included," she said. "You're single—or I'm assuming you're single—you're attractive and you're new in town. Beware." Then she frowned. "You're not interested in dating? How old are you?" she asked bluntly.

Leah smiled. "I'm fifty-one...but my age has nothing to do with me not wanting to date."

"Oh? Bad breakup?" she guessed. "I can relate. I have totally sworn off women. I will never date again."

"That bad, huh?"

Megan took a swallow of her water, contemplating telling Leah about Tammi and Erin. But then she came to her senses. Why in the world would she tell that to Leah Rollins, of all people? But she was curious about her.

"You ever been in love?"

Leah nodded. "Yes. Madly."

"Good. It's nice to know it's out there. In my experience, it doesn't exist," she said, noting the bitterness in her voice.

"So you haven't been in love, yet you've sworn off dating?"

Megan sighed. "I thought I was in love. I guess I don't know what it feels like." She met Leah's eyes, trying to decide if they were a smoky gray or a smoky blue. "What happened with you? I mean, if you were madly in love?"

"Oh. Well…"

Megan's eyes widened. "Oh, no. She died? I'm so sorry," she said quickly.

Leah grinned. "No, no. Nothing that dramatic." Then she tilted her head. "Well, I guess it was dramatic."

Megan leaned forward. "Oh, no. She went to *men*?"

Leah nodded. "Yep."

"Oh, God. That's the worst. Was she bi?"

Leah shrugged. "Well, she claimed she was straight."

"Straight?"

"Of course the five years we were together, there wasn't a straight bone in her body," she said easily.

"Oh, I hate women like that," Megan said.

Leah shrugged again. "It's in the past. But it took me a while to trust anyone after that," Then she laughed. "I'd go out with them and then I'd ask them if they were sure they were gay or if they had a secret crush on men."

Megan laughed too.

"Most thought I was crazy and wouldn't go out with me again," Leah said. "And over the years, I've found that it really wasn't worth the trouble."

"So in a roundabout way, you've sworn off women too."

"In a roundabout way, I suppose."

As they looked at each other, Megan realized that there was zero hostility between them. That was a first. Perhaps it was good that she had had to hide from Mary Beth. It gave her and Leah a chance to chat about things other than parking.

"Well, I should go," she said as she stood. "I'm late as it is." She handed over her empty water bottle. "Thank you."

"Sure."

They went back downstairs into the shop, but at the front door, Megan paused, looking in both directions down the street.

"I hope she's not in the grill waiting for me," she said. She was about to go out when she saw the door open and Nancy walked out. She shielded her eyes as she looked around, no doubt looking for Megan. Then Nancy put her phone to her ear and Megan held her own up. "Wait for it," she murmured. She answered on the first ring.

"Where are you?" Nancy demanded. "You're late."

"I'm hiding from Mary Beth," she said.

"She already left." Then Nancy laughed. "And as a warning…you might want to avoid Facebook."

Megan gritted her teeth. "Son of a bitch," she muttered as she pocketed her phone. She glanced at Leah. "Are you friends with Mary Beth?"

Leah shrugged. "Well, I hardly know her, really. I met her at the party, that's it."

Megan rolled her eyes. "On Facebook!"

"Oh. Yeah. Why?"

"Where's your phone? Bring it up," she said impatiently, waving her index finger in a circle.

Leah scrolled through a few screens, then her eyes widened. "Good Lord."

Megan snatched the phone from her. Her breath left her as she stared at a picture of herself. It was a torso shot, slightly below her hip bone up to the swell of her breast. Another centimeter and her nipple would be showing.

"Oh. My. *Freakin'*. God. She has lost her mind."

Leah took the phone from her, staring again at the picture. "Wow. Just…wow." Then she grinned. "Are you sure this is you?"

Megan slugged her in the arm. "Of course I'm sure it's me!" she snapped. "I'm being exposed—little by little—by a crazy woman!"

Leah laughed as she rubbed her arm. "So tell her you're dating someone. Surely she'll stop then."

Megan stared at her blankly. "In this town? I know we have a large gay population, but still, everybody knows everybody. You can't make up a date in this town." God knows, she would have tried already if she thought it would work.

Leah put her phone away and shrugged. "So use me."

Megan's mouth dropped open. "*What?* I don't even like you."

Again, an easy smile lit her face. "Well, I'm not crazy about you either, but hey…I'm just offering. If you want to make them stop…and besides, it'll save me from having to turn down any potential dates too."

Megan met her gaze. Was Leah serious? And would she actually consider it?

Megan pointed out the door. "I…I need to go."

CHAPTER THIRTEEN

The lunch crowd was in full swing by the time Megan finally stepped behind the bar. She'd only had to endure three exaggerated wolf whistles as she passed through the grill.

"I'll kill her," she mumbled under her breath, then she forced a smile as a man at the end of the bar raised his hand. She walked over to him. "Another beer?"

"Coors. Draft," he said before shoving an onion ring in his mouth.

She absently filled a mug and took it over to him. There were only three people eating at the bar and the other two were drinking tea. She went to the opposite end and leaned against it, letting her mind wander back to her conversation with Leah Rollins. It was a perfect solution, she admitted. If they pretended to be dating, then surely Mary Beth would back off. Surely. The problem was, would anyone actually believe that they were dating? Nancy wouldn't, that's for sure. She'd have to tell Nancy it was all a farce.

She shook her head. No. Nancy wouldn't be able to keep her mouth shut. She'd end up letting it slip—probably to Mary Beth—that they were fake dating. Or worse, she'd tell Susie and then the whole damn town would know.

If you couldn't trust your own sister with a lie, who could you trust?

If it got out that she and Leah weren't really dating, she'd never live it down.

Oh, this is a really bad idea.

She couldn't actually believe she was contemplating it in the first place. As she'd told Leah, she didn't even like her. But maybe they could pretend to date for a couple of months. Tourist season would be in full swing then...surely this crap on Facebook would die down or they'd all lose interest in it. It would be in the thick of summer, everyone would be busy. Surely they could pull it off. She stared up at the ceiling and shook her head.

"This is a really bad idea," she murmured.

"What are you mumbling about?"

She turned to Nancy and shook her head quickly. "Nothing...nothing."

"I need a margarita on the rocks, no salt and an extra spicy bloody Mary," she said.

Megan raised her eyebrows. "Extra spicy?"

Nancy shrugged. "That's what he said." Nancy sat down on one of the barstools to wait. "Why were you so late?"

"Sorry. I made breakfast at the last minute so it put me behind on my treadmill session," she said. "And I was rocking it, by the way."

"Five miles?"

"Six today," she said. "And I felt great. That is, until I saw Mary Beth when I drove up."

Nancy laughed. "She saw your SUV outside and thought you were hiding in here. She looked everywhere, including the ladies' room."

"She's insane," she said as she slid over the margarita. "I was hiding next door."

"Oh? With Leah Rollins?"

"Yeah. When I saw Mary Beth, I pulled into the first spot I found. Unfortunately, it was for Ruby's," she said with a smirk. "Leah promptly informed me that I was in a reserved spot. I'm telling you, she's obsessed with the parking situation." She didn't admit that Leah had been teasing at the time.

"Were you at least civil to her?"

"Of course I was civil. Unlike her, I'm over the whole parking thing already."

"I don't know why you don't like her. I think she's really cute. And I just love her hair."

Megan shrugged. Yeah, Leah was cute...for being over fifty. And yes, her hair was kinda unique.

"She has dreamy eyes too," Nancy added with a sigh.

"Dreamy?" She wouldn't go that far.

"Maybe I should ask her out."

Megan's eyes widened. *Oh, crap!*

But Nancy waved her hand in the air. "I'm not her type apparently. I flirted with her at the party. I flirted with her when she had lunch over here the other week. She totally ignored my hints."

"Sorry," she said as she passed across the bloody Mary after stabbing three olives on a plastic toothpick.

"Oh, well," Nancy said as she walked off.

Megan slowly shook her head. If she and Leah fake dated, Nancy would be pissed. Or hurt. Or both. Of course, if it came to her sanity or her sister...well, she could lose her sanity, but she wouldn't lose her sister...right? Maybe she should check with Leah to see if she had any interest in Nancy. That would be the logical thing to do. But Leah had already said she wasn't interested in dating anyone. And if she did like Nancy, then why would she even suggest they fake date to begin with? No... she didn't have any interest in Nancy. Poor Nancy.

"Oh, this is a really bad idea," she murmured.

CHAPTER FOURTEEN

Before Leah bought the old bookstore last fall, she'd spent nearly a week in town playing tourist. Well, snooping around the other shops, really. Before she'd even decided on Eureka Springs, she'd also gone up to Branson, but she could tell immediately that the vibe in that town wasn't for her. It catered to an older, more conservative crowd, and she'd felt out of place walking the streets there. Here, it was completely different. The staircase streets were jam-packed with lively, colorful shops. The crowds were eclectic and diverse, young mixed with old, the people watchers and free spirits, old hippies and young hipsters. She'd felt at home immediately.

But the problem remained, what type of shop did she want? Probably not the wisest thing to purchase a shop and no inventory—but she wanted a new start and she now had the time and money to make it happen. But what, exactly, did she want?

Most of the shops in town were specialized, but not all. There was a shop that sold glass and crystal, not much more.

The quilt shop. The Christmas shop, which sold all things for the holiday and not a single thing that wasn't Christmas-themed. There was a shop that sold decorative signs, both metal and wood. A shop that sold windsocks and flags. A shop for yard art and bird feeders. A gift shop for souvenirs, the T-shirt shop, the candle shop, the chocolate place, the turkey jerky place. There was even a shop she referred to as the junk shop. Some of the merchandise was duplicated from shop to shop…like T-shirts and coffee mugs, but most was unique to each shop.

What she wanted for her shop was variety. She wanted her shop to be like the town itself—diverse—with a wide range of inventory. But flipping through the catalogs she'd ordered, she realized how easy it would be to overdo it. She also realized why most shops specialized. It was much simpler.

Well, her original plan seemed logical enough, at least to her. T-shirts, wind chimes and such. By snooping around in the shops last fall, she'd gotten an idea of what the top sellers were in each place. She would collectively offer those items at her shop as well as a few things that had caught her eye in Branson, namely, wood carvings and chainsaw art. The fun part was going to be shopping for it all.

Now all she had to do was wait for Tony to finish the remodeling, which would be only a matter of days. Gordon Russell told her that her new sign for out front would be ready in about ten days…the first of May. Once the sign was up and her inventory started trickling in, Ruby's would be ready to open for business. Did she dare shoot for a June first opening?

She sighed. That, of course, was the scary part—actually opening for business. She shook her head. No, the scary part was the fear of having no customers.

* * *

Megan paused halfway between the grill and the bookstore. This is a terrible idea, she told herself once again. Terrible. But Nancy had heard that Mary Beth's next Facebook post was due out in a few days. Couple the prospect of a new picture with that of her latest date offer—Gwen Barksdale—and the terrible idea didn't seem quite as terrible. Gwen had heard "through the grapevine" that Megan was now "on the market." Gwen Barksdale was very nice. She was also sixty-five years old...her mother's age. No, the terrible idea didn't seem terrible at all from that vantage point.

Of course, now—as she contemplated going to Leah Rollins and accepting the ridiculous fake date offer—she was hesitant to actually go through with it. Because the chances were really, really good that they wouldn't be able to pull it off. Was she prepared to suffer through *that* humiliation just to avoid being exposed on Facebook by Mary Beth Sturgeon?

"Hell, yeah," she murmured as she started walking again. It did occur to her that if they were found out to be fake dating, Mary Beth might go berserk and post all of her pictures anyway, but that was a chance she'd have to take.

The front door to the bookstore stood open and she walked inside, looking around at the changes Tony had made. It hardly looked like the same place and she supposed she'd have to stop referring to it as "the bookstore."

"Hello?" she called loudly. "Leah?"

"Back here."

She walked around to where the coffee bar used to be, amazed at the transformation in the last week. With all the shelves and coffee bar gone—plus the new windows out front—the store looked much bigger than before. It was bright and airy and she wondered what kind of store Ruby's would be.

As she looked around, Leah came out of the back room. Mr. Carlton's old storage room, she remembered.

"Hey, Megan. What brings you around?" Leah asked. "Mary Beth stalking you again?"

Megan smiled briefly. "I haven't seen her, thankfully. Although Nancy's heard from Susie that Mary Beth plans her most provocative post yet."

"Can't wait," Leah teased as she wiggled her eyebrows.

Megan ignored that and motioned behind her. "What's back there? Still storage?"

"Part of it," Leah said. "I squeezed in a corner for my office. Come take a look," she offered.

Megan didn't recall there being any windows in the back that faced the alley, but now the old storage room was brightly lit by the noonday sun. Leah nodded at her unasked question.

"Yeah, I had to have windows. It took them one whole day to knock out the wall."

"Not worried about someone breaking in from the alley?" she asked.

"Well, there's no window in the part where I'll keep my inventory, but I didn't realize we had to worry about crime here."

Megan shrugged. "No, not really. But during the summer, there are lots of people in town who aren't locals, including seasonal workers," she said.

"I guess I'll take my chances," Leah said. "I don't imagine I'll have anything so expensive in the shop that someone would break in to steal it."

Megan arched an eyebrow. "What exactly is Ruby's going to be?" It was a question that had been bouncing around town for weeks. Even Susie didn't have a clue.

Leah smiled. "Yeah, well…that's kinda a work in progress," she said.

Megan's eyes widened. "Oh, my God! You don't even know, do you?"

Leah laughed. "Don't tell anyone, please. They'll think I'm crazy."

"You *are* crazy!"

"Oh, I have a plan. In fact, I was in the process of ordering stuff when you came in," Leah said, pointing to the laptop that was on top of an impeccably clean desk. "Tony's finished with everything so I'm ready to roll."

"What about tables, shelves? Display cases?" she asked. "The place is gutted."

"Already ordered. Should be in next week. Gordon Russell is going to install all of that for me, as well as a sign for out front." She looked at her questioningly. "I'm sure you didn't come over to discuss my shop though."

"Oh…well." Megan twisted her hands together, wondering if she should reconsider. But then she pictured Gwen Barksdale's face as she'd asked her out, Gwen's eyelashes fluttering seductively at her as she'd waited for Megan's answer.

"Problem?"

Megan sighed. "Gwen Barksdale asked me out."

Leah smiled. "And who is Gwen Barksdale?"

"She owns the Christmas store." Then she smiled too. "And she's sixty-five."

Leah laughed. "Wow. And you're what?"

"Thirty-nine." Megan could see that Leah was trying to keep the smile off her face.

"Well, I'm sure Gwen is very nice. When are you going out with her?"

"I'm not going out with her!" She took a deep breath. "I wanted to see if your offer was still on the table."

Leah's eyebrows rose. "What offer?"

"That… you and I," Megan said, motioning between them, "would fake date."

Leah nodded. "Oh, that offer. Actually, it's very much on the table. It seems Tony is trying to set me up with a friend of his…or a friend of his partner's," she said.

"Let me guess…Carla?"

"Yeah, that was her name. I guess we met at the party. I don't remember her."

"Jet-black hair. She owns the art gallery."

"Oh, okay, yeah," Leah nodded. "I remember her now." Leah went to the small fridge beside her desk and took out two water bottles, handing one to Megan. "So? What's the plan?"

Megan shrugged. "I don't know. A couple of things make me think that this is a very bad idea. Okay, more than a couple," she admitted. "First of all, I'm not sure Nancy will believe it.

I may have called you…well, irritating. And annoying. And a bully. And maybe a psycho crazy woman."

Leah laughed. "Yeah, that could be a problem. I think I called you annoying too."

Megan frowned. "You called *me* annoying? *Really?* The woman who put up parking signs to a shop that's not even open yet? You called *me* annoying?"

A smile played around Leah's mouth. "I did. What are your other concerns?"

"Nancy's been hinting that she might ask you out."

Leah groaned. "I like your sister fine. In fact, she's very nice. I think we could be friends."

"But?"

"But I'm not attracted to her in the least. And I've done nothing to make her think otherwise."

Megan nodded. "I know. She said you've ignored her attempts at flirting."

"Okay. So there's two concerns. What else?"

"If we don't pull this off, I'll be crucified. They'll probably take me down to the amphitheater so the whole town can gather and watch…at the stroke of midnight, no doubt."

Leah laughed out loud, then sobered as Megan narrowed her eyes at her.

"You think I'm kidding? Mary Beth will lead the parade… she'll probably have a giant poster with a naked photo of me on it."

Leah laughed again and this time, Megan joined her. "Okay, so maybe I'm exaggerating a little." Then her smile faltered. "This is a bad idea, isn't it?"

Leah shrugged. "Could be fun."

"Fun? There will be nothing fun about it. It will be stressful. But my hope is, after a month or two, everyone will be too busy with tourist season to even care about us anymore."

"That's your hope?"

"That's my hope."

CHAPTER FIFTEEN

Megan had to force herself not to glance at the door each time it opened. She refilled the cocktail napkins and pretended immense interest in the baseball game that was showing on the TV above the bar instead, all the while tapping her fingers rapidly on the counter's wooden surface.

Their plan—after much debate and a little arguing—was for Leah to pop over to the grill, early, before the dinner crowd, and ask to be seated at the bar…where Megan was conveniently working. They would pretend to visit—like normal people—and hopefully Nancy would see them, perhaps even come over to visit as well. Then, with Nancy there, Leah would ask Megan out. According to their plan, Megan would be too shocked at the proposal to find the words to decline. Leah would leave with a promise for them to get together very soon and Megan would then moan and complain to Nancy that she'd been duped into accepting.

It was a horrible plan.

"Excuse me. Can I get another beer, please?"

Megan turned and gave an apologetic smile to the man sitting down across from her. She'd totally forgotten about him.

"Sorry," she said. "Another Sam?" she asked, referring to the Samuel Adams he'd ordered earlier.

He nodded, then turned his attention to the baseball game while she pulled a cold mug from the freezer and began filling it.

"Your lucky day," Nancy said as she came over. "Instead of twelve separate drinks, they've agreed on margaritas." Then she gave Megan an evil smile. "They insist on Patrón tequila. Your favorite," she teased.

Megan groaned and stuck her tongue out. Ever since her birthday, she stayed clear of tequila. She glanced over at the loud group of women who had come in. This must be the bachelorette party that had called earlier to reserve a table.

"Who starts their bachelorette party at four in the afternoon?" she asked. She placed the beer in front of the man and snatched up the bills he'd placed there. "Thanks," she said with a quick smile before turning back to Nancy. "Where are they from?"

"They've got two of Steve's cottages booked for the weekend," Nancy said. "I think they're from Tulsa."

Megan grabbed the bottle of Patrón, trying to ignore the smell, when Nancy leaned closer. "Guess who just came in."

Megan glanced toward the door, her heart thumping nervously in her chest.

Yeah, it was a bad plan.

"You think she came for dinner?" Nancy asked. "Oh, she's coming over," she whispered excitedly.

A very, very bad plan.

"Hi, ladies," Leah said as she sat down. "I know it's a little early for dinner, but I missed lunch," she explained.

Megan ignored her as she continued making the margaritas.

"Glad you came by," Nancy said with an exaggerated smile. "I've got a huge table," she said, motioning with her head to the laughing group of women, "but if you'll give me a second, I'll bring a menu right over."

"No hurry," Leah said. "I'm sure Megan can keep me company."

"Sure," Megan said. "We'll discuss parking or something."

Nancy laughed and touched Leah's arm. "Oh, you two try to get along. I'll be right back," she said as she took the first tray of drinks.

As soon as she left, Leah shrugged. "Bad timing, huh?"

Megan sighed. "Bad plan." Nancy had her back to them and Megan turned back to Leah. "She's going to be hurt," she said quietly. "I hate doing this to her."

"Whether we do this or not, Megan, I'm not interested in your sister. Would it hurt her any less if I flat-out rejected her?"

"I suppose not," she said as she placed the tenth out of twelve margaritas on a serving tray. "You want something to drink?"

"Water is fine," Leah said.

Megan reached in the cooler for a bottle and placed it in front of her. "Here she comes," she whispered.

"They're a rowdy bunch," Nancy said. "Bachelorette party," she explained to Leah. Then she snapped her fingers. "Oh, I meant to get you a menu. Be right back."

Megan shook her head as she hurried off. It was a bad plan. "Maybe we should reconsider," she said to Leah.

Leah shrugged. "Look, I don't mind saying 'no' to potential dates, but I'd rather not alienate a large portion of the lesbian population in town by appearing to be standoffish." Their eyes met. "But it's your call," she said. "I'm not the one whose photo keeps appearing on Facebook."

Megan put the last of the drinks on the tray, then slid it over as Nancy came back. Nancy placed the menu beside Leah and took the tray.

"Give me just a second," Nancy said as she hurried off.

Megan sighed again. "So...what shall we pretend to visit about? Got all your inventory ordered yet? Have any idea what your theme will be?"

Leah smiled. "Are you trying to figure out my plan so you can share it with Susie?"

Megan smiled. "She's not the only one who's dying to know," she said. "Nearly every local who comes in here asks about it."

"Why is everyone so curious?"

"Well, competition is one reason, but mainly, you've been so secretive about it, you have everyone guessing."

Leah laughed. "I've only been secretive about it because I don't know. Or didn't. I kinda have a clue now."

"But you're not ready to share?"

"No. You'll have to wait."

Nancy came back over and sat down next to Leah with a heavy sigh. "Sorry that took so long. They ordered appetizers." She smiled at Leah. "What about you? Want something to snack on?"

"No. I think I'm going to try your pesto burger today," Leah said. "With onion rings, of course."

"Medium well," Megan supplied, then shrugged as both Nancy and Leah stared at her. "That's what you had the last time."

"Since when do you remember orders?" Nancy asked.

Yeah, Megan…since when do you remember orders?

She bit her lip. "Or was it medium rare? I forget," she said lamely as she arched an eyebrow at Leah, who was trying to hide a smile.

"Let's go with medium well," Leah said. "And I suppose I should get this to go, Nancy. I've got some work to finish this afternoon."

"Oh, that's too bad. I was hoping you'd stay and visit," Nancy said.

"You seem pretty busy," Leah said. "And I imagine the dinner crowd will be coming soon."

"Yes, it'll pick up very shortly," Nancy said as she stood. "Well, maybe another time."

When Nancy walked over to the table of boisterous women, Leah leaned closer. "So I'm thinking you should just tell her that I asked you out."

"*What?* No! That's not the plan. She's supposed to be here when you ask me," Megan said.

"Well, I don't think that's a very good plan," Leah said.

"I tried to tell you that."

"No...this plan was your idea. I wanted to—"

"Are you kidding me? This was *your* idea! I told you this wouldn't work!"

Leah threw up her hands. "Whatever. Just tell her I asked you out."

"And then what?"

"And then what what?"

Megan took a step back as Nancy again came over.

"Your burger will be right out, Leah." Nancy turned to her. "Coors on draft and a rum and Diet Coke."

"Miss? Can we order?"

Megan turned, finding a couple sitting down at the end of the bar waving at her. She smiled at them and nodded. "Be right there," she said as she filled a mug with draft beer.

"I'm keeping you from your job," Leah said. "Maybe I should—"

"No, no, you're fine," Nancy said, putting a hand on Leah's arm. "Megan has a problem multitasking sometimes."

Between the bar starting to fill up and Nancy staying glued to Leah's side, Megan had no more time to discuss this so-called plan that was going haywire. When there was finally a break, she walked over to Leah, about to tell her that they should scrap the whole thing when Nancy came back with her burger.

She stood in complete shock when Leah looked at her and gave a very subtle wink, her words just loud enough for Nancy to hear.

"So...it's a date. I look forward to it."

Megan stared, speechless, as Leah handed Nancy some money and left after telling Nancy to "keep the change." Time seemed to stand still as Nancy slowly turned, her eyebrows raised expectantly.

"Well?"

"What?"

"*What?*" Nancy tilted her head. "It's a date?"

Oh, it was a really bad plan.

"We're…she wants…well…she may have asked…I think…"

Cheers erupted from Nancy's bachelorette party, distracting her. Megan took that opportunity to hurry to the other side of the bar, hoping someone—anyone—needed a refill.

When Clint showed up at six to take over bar duty, Megan quickly went to the front, intending to relieve Patty as hostess.

Patty looked at her suspiciously. "I normally have to beg you for a break."

"That is so not true," Megan said, feigning insult. "Go help bus tables or something."

"That's my break? Busing tables?"

Megan sighed. "I'm avoiding Nancy, okay?"

Patty shook her head. "I don't even want to know. Call me when it's safe to come back."

It was another boisterous dinner crowd and conversation and laughter drowned out the music that was playing. As was the norm, she and Nancy wore several hats and after letting Patty get back to her hostess duties, Megan took a turn serving. She and Nancy had no time to talk, but she could see by the look in Nancy's eyes that she'd have some explaining to do.

As the evening wore on and the crowd thinned, she joined Clint at the bar where it was still mostly packed. On weekdays, they stopped serving dinner at nine but the bar stayed open until ten. Weekends during the summer months, they had extended hours, especially when they had live music on the patio. Those were the most profitable nights, when the place would stay filled until midnight, but those were also the most exhausting nights.

"Nice crowd for a Thursday," Nancy said later as they settled down at the bar for an after-work drink.

Megan nodded. "Yes. Busy."

"So…a date?"

Megan sighed. She hadn't had time to rehearse a response, she'd been so busy. Now, her tired brain fumbled to come up with anything suitable.

"She...she mentioned having dinner is all," Megan said weakly.

"With you?"

Megan nodded.

"And you accepted?"

"I was so shocked that she even asked, I couldn't think of an excuse," she said.

Nancy's stare was intense. "So all this pretending that you found her annoying and...and irritating—you secretly liked her!"

"I don't like her! She *is* irritating," Megan insisted.

"Then why didn't you say no?"

"I told you...I was too shocked. In fact, I'll probably go over there and tell her no tomorrow."

Nancy looked at her accusingly. "I think you do like her. Pretending to hide over there from Mary Beth. It was just an excuse to—"

"I *was* hiding from Mary Beth!"

But Nancy shook her head. "I guess I used the wrong approach with Leah. Instead of being nice to her, I should have been mean and snippy, like you."

"I wasn't mean and snippy," Megan said. "Well...maybe a little. But—"

"Forget it," Nancy said dismissively. "Go on your date with her. She obviously wasn't interested in me. God knows I gave her enough hints."

Megan bit her lip. Whose brilliant idea was this, anyway? She blamed Leah, of course. She would have never suggested they fake date if Leah hadn't mentioned it.

"I'm sorry," she said. "I should tell her no and you should ask her out." There. She was offering. It was gallant. Her conscience was cleared.

"Oh, Megan, it doesn't matter," Nancy said with a shake of her head. "Go out with her. I can't imagine what the two of you will talk about though. Other than argue over parking spots. Unless that, too, was just an excuse to see her."

She groaned silently. *Whose idea was this?*

CHAPTER SIXTEEN

Leah watched with amusement as Megan paced across the floor in her shop. Megan was not happy with her, as she'd expected. In fact, she wouldn't have been surprised to find Megan pounding on her door last night instead of early this morning.

"And then she accused me of secretly liking you!"

"That *is* terrible."

Megan glared at her. "We had a plan," she said again for the third time. "Not a very good plan, but a plan. And it did not involve *me* having to explain a date to Nancy."

"As I said, your plan involved—"

"*Our* plan," Megan corrected.

"Regardless," Leah said. "The plan called for you and me to visit first, then have Nancy come over." She shrugged. "Since she was already at the bar when I got there, I thought I would improvise."

Megan rubbed her forehead. "She's hardly speaking to me."

Leah held up her hands. "What do you want me to do?"

"I don't know."

"Look at it this way," she said. "At least she believes us. You were worried she'd suspect this was a fake date, as you call it."

"I know, I know," Megan said. "I'm sorry."

Leah's eyebrows shot up. "You're actually apologizing? What's wrong with you?"

Again...a glare. "Have I told you that I don't really like you?"

Leah smiled. "Yeah. A couple of times already."

"God, this was a stupid idea," Megan muttered. "I can't believe I let you talk me into this."

Leah laughed. "I think you're twisting this around a little. Remember Mary Beth? Your problem, not mine."

"And that's the only reason I'm going through with this. The sooner she hears about it, the better chance I have of saving what little dignity I have left."

"So when are we expecting the next Facebook posting?"

Megan put her hands on her hips. "I think you're enjoying my plight," she accused.

Leah couldn't hide her smile. "Well, you have to admit, the photos are really good. I mean, if you like pictures of semi-naked women, that is."

Megan gave her a fake smile. "I'm glad you find this humorous. I can't wait for the day that I get to break up with you!"

Leah laughed. "Now is that any way to start a new relationship? Already picturing the end?"

Megan blew out her breath and leaned her head back, staring up at the ceiling. "Okay, back to the real issue," she said. "Where should we go on our first date?"

"Well, if you want to be seen by locals and get the word out, where would you go?"

Megan smiled. "You'd go to the Phenix Grill, of course."

"Okay, so that's out. What else?"

"We could go to El Gallo," Megan said. "A lot of locals go there too."

Leah frowned. "Tex-Mex?"

"Yeah, they're really good. Best in town."

Leah shook her head. "I'm from California. I don't do Tex-Mex."

"What are you talking about? Their enchiladas are great."

"It's not even real Mexican food," she said. "It's something they made up in Austin or somewhere."

Megan frowned at her. "Of course it's real Mexican food. I mean, which state has a longer border with Mexico?"

"Oh, come on. That's what you're going on? We practically invented Mexican food."

Megan held her hands up. "Okay, okay. Whatever," she said. "No Mexican food."

"What about the Burger Barn?"

"Are you out of your mind? That's our competition for burgers. I can't be seen there."

Leah shrugged. "They weren't very good anyway. Prices are way cheaper than you, though."

"You get what you pay for." Then a slight narrowing of eyes. "You went there already?"

"Yeah. You know, trying out different places in town," she said.

Megan paused. "Well, okay, but you can't ever go again. Besides, they're not very friendly there."

"No? You mean, as opposed to…say…you?"

Megan's eyes widened in shock. "I'm *very* friendly," she insisted.

"The first time we met, you stormed in here, yelled at me, wadded up my note and threw it at me," Leah reminded her.

"What do you expect? You took away my parking spot and you weren't even open yet! You're *still* not open!"

As they stood there staring at each other, Megan slowly shook her head. "This is a really bad idea, isn't it?"

"Oh, it'll be fine," she said, even though she tended to agree with Megan. It would be a miracle if they pulled it off. "We probably shouldn't argue in public though."

Megan smiled. A rather sweet smile, Leah had to admit. "Well, if you would just agree with me, then we wouldn't have to argue."

Leah laughed. "Spoken like a true girlfriend."

"Relationships would be so much easier that way if one simply gave in to the other…all the time."

"As long as you're the one getting her way?"

Megan laughed. "Of course."

Leah was about to ask if that had been one of the problems in her failed relationships, but she remembered she wasn't supposed to know about them. She'd promised Nancy she wouldn't say anything. So she changed the subject back to their date.

"How about that romantic place Mary Beth wanted to take you to?"

"Craig's? Fancy schmancy dining," she said. "Mostly tourists. Locals rarely go there."

"Why? Is it not good? The food at the kickoff party was pretty good."

"Oh, no. Excellent food. But expensive. Locals can't afford it!" Megan said with a laugh.

"So if we went there, it would be a big deal?"

"Oh, yeah. Locals go there only for special occasions or if they're celebrating something. Craig is friends with Susie. He'll probably call her while we're there. By the time we leave, it'll be all over town that we had dinner together," Megan said. She rubbed her hands together conspiratorially. "Good plan."

"See? We agreed on something. That wasn't too hard, was it?"

"No, it wasn't. I hate dressing up though," Megan said.

Leah wrinkled up her nose. "We have to dress up? That may be a problem. I ditched all of my suits and dressy clothes when I retired."

Megan tilted her head. "Do you have black jeans?"

Leah nodded. "I actually have two pair."

"Add a nice blouse, maybe a sweater. It's still cool enough."

"Okay. I'll see what I can do. It would be kinda embarrassing if he wouldn't allow us in on our first date," she said with a laugh.

"He wouldn't dare."

CHAPTER SEVENTEEN

"So you're going to Craig's, huh? And *that's* what you're wearing?"

Megan looked down at her neatly pressed khaki slacks and the shoes that hurt her feet. "What's wrong with this?"

"A sweater vest? Is that even in style?"

Megan smoothed her hands over the soft wool of the navy vest she wore. It was her favorite and she admitted she hadn't worn it in a couple of years but still, she thought it looked nice with the gingham blouse. Regardless, she wasn't going to argue with Nancy about it. She was stressed enough about the prospect of her first date with Leah.

"Wow…you look nice," Eileen said from the doorway. "What's the occasion?"

Megan gave Nancy a smirk. "See? I look nice."

"She's got a hot date," Nancy said. "If you can believe that."

"Oh, my God! You're finally going out with Mary Beth?"

"Of course not!" she snapped. "I'm not insane."

"Leah Rollins, from next door," Nancy supplied.

Eileen frowned. "The woman you called a 'parking space whore'?"

Megan smiled sheepishly. "Did I really use that term?"

"Among others," Eileen said.

"Apparently, she's had a secret crush on her the whole time," Nancy said.

"I do not! She asked *me* out, not the other way around," Megan said. "I don't even like her."

"Then why didn't you turn her down?"

Megan rolled her eyes. "Again with this? I thought I'd explained."

"Yeah, yeah. You were too shocked to say no. Now you've got to suffer through a date with her at Craig's," Nancy said sarcastically.

"Unless we're too busy for me to skip out tonight," she said, knowing they weren't. Mondays were always their slowest days.

"No. You go have fun," Eileen said. Then she grinned. "I wonder who's going to tell Mary Beth that you have a date."

Megan feigned ignorance. "Why would someone feel the need to tell her?"

"Oh, I don't know...could it be that she's threatening to post a fully naked picture of you unless you go out with her?"

Megan squared her shoulders. "I am not going to be blackmailed into a date. Especially not with a crazy woman who has a naked picture of me!"

A loud clearing of the throat had the three of them all turning to look toward the office door. Leah was leaning casually against the jamb, smiling.

"Am I interrupting anything?"

Megan took a few seconds to look her over, noting that the smoky black and gray shirt matched her hair perfectly. Leah had also taken her advice and worn black jeans. A black leather belt wound around her trim waist and Megan finally raised her eyes, meeting Leah's.

"No. Come in."

Leah nodded, then glanced at Nancy with a smile. "Hello, Nancy."

Megan wondered if Nancy would be cool to her or not. Apparently Leah's charming smile melted some of the frost.

"Hi, Leah. About time someone dragged this one out on a date," Nancy said. "You two have fun. I should get back out there."

Nancy gave a quick smile to Megan as she passed by, but Megan knew it was forced. Eileen stood by uncomfortably and Megan finally found her manners.

"Leah, this is Eileen. She actually runs the place," she said with a smile. "Or at least she thinks she does," she added.

Eileen laughed as she shook Leah's hand. "Nice to finally meet you, Leah. And she's right, of course. I do run the place." She winked at Megan and mouthed "she's cute" as she left them.

When they were alone, Leah raised her eyebrows. "Nervous?"

"Yes. You?"

Leah smiled easily. "No. I'm looking forward to a nice dinner and an expensive bottle of wine." She motioned to the door. "Shall we?"

Leah's relaxed attitude put her at ease…at least a little. She nodded, then preceded her out the door.

"You look nice," she tossed back over her shoulder.

* * *

"So Nancy didn't have a problem with you getting away tonight?" she asked after they'd been seated.

"Mondays are fairly quiet," Megan said.

"Same over here, it seems," Leah said as she looked around. There were only three other tables occupied.

"Mondays are slow, at least until summer," Megan said. "And I think Nancy's over the whole date thing anyway. At least she's speaking to me again."

"Maybe I should go over for lunch tomorrow and chat with her. Just, you know, as friends."

"Give it a few days," Megan suggested. Then she leaned forward slightly. "Craig is coming over," she whispered.

"Well, well. Imagine my surprise to find you here, Megan Phenix," he said dramatically as he bowed at the waist. "To what do I owe the pleasure?"

Megan waved at Leah. "Have you met Leah Rollins? She owns the shop next to our grill," she said.

Craig reached out a hand, squeezing hers gently. "I remember seeing you at the kickoff party, but I didn't get a chance to chat," he said. "Pleased to meet you, Leah."

"Thank you. I was told that this was the place to come to if you were trying to make an impression on a first date," she said as casually as she could.

He put a hand to his chest. "Oh, my. A date?" His glance slid to Megan. "Well…this *is* news." A big smile lit his face as he turned back to Leah. "With your permission, if you would allow me to select the wine…I have a special bottle for this very occasion."

Leah's smile faltered. "Do you by chance have a California wine?"

"California," he mocked. "No, I only serve the best wine, love. French. I have a beautiful blend of cabernet sauvignon that I have been saving. From the Bordeaux region. Allow me to present it to you tonight."

"Very well," she said. "Thank you."

Megan was smiling as he left. "You really are snobbish about your California wine, huh? You should have seen your face when he said French."

Leah nodded. "Guilty. But I'll try to choke it down." She lowered her voice. "I detect a slight British accent from him… sort of."

Megan laughed. "No. Craig just considers himself royalty in town and his accent gets a little better each year. He's from South Carolina." She laughed again. "You should have heard it when he first started speaking this way. It was hilarious."

"So there are quite a few…characters in town, huh?"

Megan nodded. "Characters is a nice way of putting it. And some are bordering on eccentric, yes."

"Well, it shouldn't ever be boring, I guess." She opened the menu, surprised at how limited it was—lobster, smoked salmon, prime rib, roasted duck and Cornish game hens. However, each entrée came with four or five side dishes.

"The Cornish hens are really good," Megan said. "I love the wild rice and mushroom sauce."

"I thought the locals didn't eat here," Leah reminded her.

"I've been a couple of times. Whenever our parents come to town, we usually bring them here. They get sick of eating burgers at our place."

"I haven't really looked your menu over. You have more than burgers, I assume. Tony told me to try the chicken-fried steak," she said.

"The chicken-fried steak is popular, but burgers are our specialty," Megan said. "And Johnny makes a wonderful marinade for rib eyes and fillets, if you're in the mood for a good steak."

Craig returned with a tuxedoed waiter at his side. He placed a silver tray between them containing six delectable-looking mushrooms.

"Stuffed mushrooms," Craig said. "I know Megan has a fondness for them. Tonight, I have brought you three varieties to try—a spinach and feta cheese, a very savory crab and a spicy sausage." He clapped his hands three times and another waiter appeared, placing a candle between them and two wineglasses. Craig lit the candle as the waiter added just the proper amount of wine to each glass. "This wine is simply spectacular, you're going to love it," Craig said. "Leave the bottle for them, Randal."

"Of course," the waiter said as he bowed slightly before taking his leave.

"Now…may I suggest the prime rib this evening," Craig said. "I have a beautiful creamed spinach to go with it, as well as lightly grilled asparagus spears and herb-roasted potatoes and, of course, the traditional Yorkshire pudding."

Leah nodded. "Sounds wonderful." She glanced at Megan. "Okay with you?"

"Yes. Thanks, Craig." She reached for a mushroom treat. "And thanks for these."

"My pleasure, ladies," he said. "Enjoy."

As Megan moaned after her first bite of the crab-stuffed mushroom, Leah took one of the sausage mushrooms. It was surprisingly crispy on top and the flavor was indeed spicy.

"Nice," she said as she finished off the small appetizer.

"Try the crab," Megan said as she took one of the spinach and feta. "I could eat a whole plate of those."

Leah had to agree. The crab was light and delicate, topped with bread-crusted cheese. She tasted a hint of dill in the sauce.

"Yeah, these are good."

"Johnny is a whiz with flavors and he's tried to duplicate these for me, but it's not quite the same," Megan said.

"That's the second time you've mentioned Johnny," she said.

"Oh, he's our chef," Megan said with a laugh. "We hired him as a fry cook when we first opened, but it soon became apparent that Nancy and I were only in his way."

"So when you first started the grill, you were going to cook?"

Megan shrugged. "Burgers. How hard could it be?" She took the last sausage mushroom. "But anyone can do a plain old burger. For instance, the Burger Barn."

"Definitely a plain old burger."

"Right. But Johnny was creative. He came up with all the different varieties of burgers. And it's not just the same burger with different condiments and toppings," Megan said. "Our patties are hand-formed and he actually uses different seasonings for each variety, making them unique from the others."

Leah nodded. "So you have burgers and steaks. What else?"

"We have a couple of grilled chicken entrées," Megan said. "And we have lunch specials, which he'll whip up and when it's gone, it's gone. His grandmother's meatloaf recipe is my favorite," she said. "He also makes a really nice lasagna. And during the winter months, he'll usually make chicken and dumplings at least once a week."

"So he does most of your cooking then?"

"He's in charge of the kitchen staff and he's bossy as hell, but we'd be lost without him." She smiled. "And, of course, he knows it."

"I'm assuming his salary reflects that?" Leah guessed.

"Believe it or not, the Burger Barn tried to steal him from us, among others in town. So yes, we keep him happy." Megan picked up her wineglass, which neither of them had tasted yet. "Do you think it's safe to drink?" she teased.

"Give it a try and let me know," she said with a smile.

"I told you before, I wouldn't be able to tell the difference." Megan took a sip and nodded. "Nice. I think."

Leah followed suit and had to admit that the wine was indeed very nice. She nodded her approval. "Not bad for French wine," she conceded.

Megan motioned for Leah to take the lone remaining mushroom. "So tell me about Aunt Ruby."

"Are you curious about the shop or—"

"No. Well, yes. But if we're going to pretend to date, we need to at least know something about the other, don't you think? I have a feeling Nancy will question me."

Leah nodded. "Fair enough. I'll tell you about Aunt Ruby…if you'll tell me why you drank too much tequila on your birthday." She saw the hesitation in Megan's eyes, but she finally nodded.

"Okay. But you first," Megan said.

Leah paused. "I thought today was the day Mary Beth was posting another picture," she said.

"That's what Nancy said. I assume she got word of our date and held off." Megan waved her hand in the air. "Or else she got word of our date and is so pissed, she's going to post the full body shot. In that case, I'll have to kill her." A quick smile. "And a good girlfriend would come visit me in prison."

Leah laughed. "Let's hope it doesn't come to that. Are you ever going to tell me how she got a naked picture of you?"

"I thought I had," Megan said. "Birthday? Woke up naked?"

Leah nodded. "Too much tequila. Why don't you tell me about it?"

"I thought you were going to tell me about Aunt Ruby?"

"Your story will be so much more entertaining though."

"Maybe for you," Megan said dryly.

"Come on," Leah urged. "Tell me."

Megan sighed. "Nancy planned a surprise birthday party at Mary Beth's house. Someone brought a bottle of Patrón. I got a phone call from the Wicked Witch. It went downhill from there."

"The Wicked Witch would be...an ex?" she asked nonchalantly. "Is she the reason you've sworn off women?"

"Erin. Yes, she's the second reason," Megan said. She took a sip from her wine before continuing. "Tammi was the first reason. I managed eight years before Erin charmed her way into a date." She made a face. "I must have been insane to go out with her."

"How long were you with Tammi?"

"Too damn long."

"Come on," Leah said. "Give me the gory details."

Megan sighed. "Tammi and I were together for four years. Or at least, I *thought* we were together."

"Ah. So she cheated on you."

Megan nodded. "Friends tried to warn me. Nancy told me on several occasions that she'd heard Tammi was seen out with other women," Megan said. "I never believed them. There wasn't ever anything suspicious. She came home when she was supposed to, there were never late nights out where she supposedly had to work late."

"So you confronted her or what?"

Megan met her gaze and smiled. "It's our first date. Should we really be discussing my ex?"

"Absolutely," she said. "If I ever want to cheat on you, maybe I'll learn something," she teased.

Megan leaned forward. "If you ever cheat on me, I'll kill you."

Leah laughed quietly. "Should I be concerned? That's the second time tonight you've threatened to kill someone."

Megan sighed again. "I have terrible luck with women. Tammi cheated on me throughout our four years together. Erin…we were only dating for six months. Apparently, two months into it, she was already seeing someone else." Megan's shoulders sagged. "I'm cursed. Or else I have some serious flaws that make my girlfriends want to cheat on me."

"If you had serious flaws, wouldn't it just be easier for them to break up with you?"

Megan gave her a fake smile. "It must be my glowing personality that keeps them around."

"Well, you are kinda growing on me," Leah said truthfully.

"That's good to know."

Leah motioned between them. "This is where you're supposed to say I'm growing on you too."

Megan's smile was genuine this time. "Well, we haven't argued yet this evening. I guess we're making progress." Megan leaned her elbows on the table. "So? Aunt Ruby?"

Leah shrugged. "Not a whole lot to tell. She was my dad's aunt…the old spinster woman in the family, as my grandmother liked to call her. But she wasn't really a spinster," she said.

Megan nodded. "Closeted lesbian?"

"Yes. So closeted, in fact, no one had a clue. She came out to me years ago though. I was still in college," she said. "Anyway, it was a shock to me and everyone else to learn after she died that she was quite wealthy. While I knew she dabbled in real estate, I had no idea she was as proficient as she was." Leah sipped from her wine. "And…like everyone else, I was shocked to find out I was the only beneficiary to her estate."

"Wow," Megan said. "Who all did that piss off?"

Leah laughed. "My cousins, mostly. My brothers are both younger than me and didn't know her at all," she said. "My parents are retired and they're very comfortable so there was no animosity there. I did offer to share with my father since she was his aunt, but he said if she wanted him to have her money, she'd have left him some."

"So you took the money and ran?"

Leah nodded. "After I was assured that the lawsuit my cousins filed was going nowhere, I quit my job."

"Computers, you said?"

Leah nodded. "Software engineer. I think I learned to write code before I learned my alphabet," she said with a smile. "My parents were both in the business," she explained. "They moved to San Jose when the tech industry exploded there."

Megan nodded. "I see. And will our relationship suffer when you discover that I'm about as far from a computer whiz as they come?"

Leah smiled. "I lived and breathed computers for most of my life. Would it shock you to know that I rarely even use one now? I mean, don't get me wrong, I have two laptops and an iPad, but I don't do much more than Internet browsing."

"I can relate, I guess," Megan said. "Since we've had the grill, our kitchen at home gets very little use. Occasionally, I'll have the urge to cook breakfast, but usually not."

"I don't suppose you're home for meals anyway."

"No. The grill is closed Mondays and Tuesdays during January and February, so if we do cook, those are the only days."

"I guess I didn't realize you and Nancy lived together," she said.

Megan nodded. "We have a house up above town. It's perfect for us. We each have a master bedroom and bath and only share the kitchen and living room," she said.

"Nancy is older than you, obviously," Leah said. "How much?"

"She's forty-seven, so eight years," Megan said. "Closer to your age than mine."

"Are you trying to set us up?" Leah asked in a quiet voice.

Megan shrugged. "I feel bad. I mean, I told you she wanted to ask you out."

Leah held up her hand. "I know. But...I'm not interested in that. I don't want to hurt her feelings any more than you do, but regardless if they think you and I are dating or not, I'm not going to go out with her."

"I know. I only wish—"

But she stopped when Craig came over, two waiters trailing behind him with trays loaded with food.

"The prime rib is *exceptional*," Craig said as he motioned for the waiters to serve them. He eyed the bottle of wine, then proceeded to add to their glasses. "It was to your liking, yes?"

"For a French wine, it's very good," Leah said with a nod. "Thank you."

Craig scooped up the empty platter where the mushrooms had been and bowed slightly at the waist. "Enjoy your meal, ladies. If you have room for dessert, I have an apple pie that I've just pulled from the oven."

"Thank you, Craig. Everything looks delicious," Megan said.

Craig winked at her. "I'm simply pleased that you came here tonight for your special date, Megan. I hope you'll make it a regular occurrence."

"I guess that depends on Leah," Megan said with a smile.

"Of course," he said as he turned to her. "I look forward to seeing you again."

Leah gave him a subtle nod, and he bowed once again and left them in peace.

"He's a bit over the top," Megan said. "I imagine the town is already buzzing with the news that we're here."

"But that's a good thing, right?"

"As long as Mary Beth doesn't crash the dinner, yes."

Leah touched her prime rib with her fork, amazed at the tenderness. "No need for a knife," she said.

Megan had beaten her to it and was already taking a bite. "God...this is good," she murmured.

Leah had to agree. In fact, everything was good, although she wasn't crazy about the creamed spinach. Their conversation was replaced with quiet moans and the occasional meeting of glances across the table, the candlelight flickering between them in the subdued lighting. It was a romantic setting, as Megan had predicted. Music played in the background, barely loud enough to be heard. Conversations at the other tables were muted as nearly everyone seemed absorbed in their own meals.

If she was indeed on a very first date and trying to make an impression, this would have been the spot she'd have chosen.

"Mary Beth must have good taste if this is where she planned to bring you," Leah said. "I'm quite impressed."

"Perhaps if you see her, you could thank her," Megan said with a smirk.

Leah took a sip of her wine, watching as Megan did the same. "She and Nancy are friends? I mean, if she got her to host your birthday party and all."

"I suppose they are."

"Yet they've never dated?"

Megan shook her head. "When we first moved here, Nancy dated a little, but really, it's limited. There's a large gay population, but quite a few are already coupled up."

"So her reasons for not dating are different than yours," she stated.

"Nancy was a late bloomer," Megan said with a smile. "She was married to a man for nearly ten years."

"Really? No kids?"

"No. And I always suspected she was gay, but I never said anything and of course, she was always supportive of me," Megan said. "But really, I wasn't shocked when she told me she was leaving her husband. Our parents, however...well, it took them a little while to get used to having two lesbian daughters."

"No other siblings?"

"No. But they're fine with it now and we're close. In fact, they come down quite often during the summer months, and twice a year they stay a week or more. They're coming in June to stay and then they usually come in October for the fall colors," Megan said.

Leah grinned. "Well, I look forward to meeting them. That is, if we're still dating in June."

Megan nodded. "What about you? You mentioned younger brothers."

"I have two. Pete and Lance."

Megan frowned. "Leah, Pete and Lance? Why didn't Pete warrant an L name?"

Leah smiled quickly. "Oh, he did. Lawrence. My dad's name is Lawrence, although everyone calls him Larry. My brother's name is Lawrence Peter. I think he was about eight when he refused to answer to Lawrence any longer and insisted we call him Pete."

"I see. And are they still in California?"

"They are. Both in the LA area and both are dentists."

"Really? No wonder you have such perfect teeth."

Leah gave an exaggerated smile, showing off her teeth. "Thanks."

CHAPTER EIGHTEEN

Megan strolled quietly beside Leah, admitting that it had been a good idea to walk to dinner. Leah's excuse had been that they'd be seen by more people even though Megan suspected Leah thought it would be scandalous to drive three blocks instead of walk.

"Good way to work off dinner," Leah said, breaking the silence.

"I'm not usually one to have dessert, but that pie was delicious."

Leah nudged her arm playfully. "The pie or the ice cream?"

"Okay. Mostly the ice cream," she said with a smile. "Thank you for dinner. When no one is watching, I'll pay you for half."

"No, no. My treat," Leah said. "You can pay next time."

"Great! How about Tex-Mex?"

"Determined to get me into that place, aren't you."

"Actually, I'm so full right now, I can't even think about it," she said. "But I suppose we do need a plan." She turned to Leah. "Maybe breakfast one morning?"

"You know, it doesn't always have to involve a meal," Leah said.

"I know. But I'm limited on when I can get away from the grill. Mondays and Tuesdays are really the only nights that are slow. Of course, once summer hits, even those aren't really all that slow."

"What about Nancy? Does she get a night off sometimes?"

Megan shook her head. "We don't normally take nights off. That's one reason we close for a couple of days during January and February."

"All work and no play?"

"Well, to be honest, it's not a necessity that we both be there every night. The people working for us have been with us for years and we trust them. It's just that neither Nancy nor I have a personal life," she said. "Our social life revolves around the grill."

"Okay. So maybe I'll have to hang out at the grill every once in a while," Leah said. "I heard a rumor that you have live bands some nights on the outdoor patio."

"Yes. Summer. We start in June. And don't worry…it's not every night," she said with a laugh.

"Think it'll keep me up?"

"You may be thankful you put your bedroom on the opposite side of your apartment," she said. "Although we don't go late. Normally, nine to eleven." She paused when they reached the bookstore, intending to bid Leah goodnight, but Leah kept walking toward the grill.

"Should I walk you inside?"

"Dropping me off at the front door will be sufficient," she said.

They stopped and turned, facing each other, both with slight smiles on their faces. Leah surprised her by taking her hand and swinging it casually between them.

"I enjoyed the evening," Leah said. "And hopefully word has already spread around town that we were out."

"Me too," she said truthfully. "And I have no doubt that it has. In fact, I imagine Nancy will have already had a call from Mary Beth."

Leah nodded, then leaned closer and touched her lips lightly to Megan's cheek, barely brushing the corner of her mouth. Megan was too shocked to protest and when Leah dropped her hand, it fell uselessly to her side as she stared at Leah, unblinking.

"Goodnight, Megan."

Megan nodded weakly as she watched Leah walk away. She finally blinked several times, then shook her head to clear it. *No, no, no, no.* Kissing was not a part of the deal. *Jesus*...what was Leah thinking?

She sighed. What was *she* thinking when she agreed to this? Fake dating did *not* mean fake kissing. And as soon as she had her wits about her, she'd let Leah know that!

Of course, her worries over Leah and her kissing vanished as soon as she walked into the grill and was met with wolf whistles and clapping. She plastered a smile on her face as she marched into the office, finding Nancy and Eileen giggling like schoolgirls as they stared at Nancy's phone. They both looked up guiltily as Megan glared at them.

She held her hand out. "Give me the phone."

Nancy couldn't contain her laughter. "You're going to kill her."

"No doubt."

And there she was, at the top of the Facebook newsfeed, sprawled out in Mary Beth's bed. To her, it was obvious that the photo was staged. She was, after all, passed out. To Mary Beth's credit, the sheet did cover all her important parts—mostly. However, the only thing covering her left breast was a shadow.

"It's...it's a *great* shot," Eileen said. "Have you considered modeling?"

Megan glared at her. "Have you considered a new job?"

Nancy laughed. "Oh, Megan, lighten up. It's all in fun."

"Fun? There is nothing *fun* about it."

Nancy waved her protest away. "So? How was the date?"

"It was nice," she said. "We managed to make it through dinner without arguing."

Nancy smiled. "And the prime rib?"

Megan raised an eyebrow. "How do you know what we ate?"

"Oh, come on. Craig called Susie. He couldn't wait to get the news out."

Megan had to hide her smile. Great! Their plan worked to perfection. Telling Susie was as good as taking out an ad in the newspaper. She did wonder, though, if that was what prompted Mary Beth to post the latest picture.

"I should have known Craig couldn't wait to broadcast it," she said, feigning disdain.

"Mary Beth called me too," Nancy continued.

"Oh, great. So she knows too?"

"She's very hurt," Nancy said.

Megan held up the phone. "And I'm not?" She narrowed her eyes threateningly. "We are a litigious society. Only my sense of community is keeping me from contacting an attorney," she said.

"Oh, please. Is it her fault you had too much tequila and ended up in her bed?"

Megan pointed her finger at Nancy. "No! It's *your* fault I ended up in her bed!"

"Well, I find the whole situation hilarious," Eileen said as she headed to the door. "We haven't had this much fun in town since the Coopers and the Byrds were having an affair with each other's spouse. Now that was funny."

"Why do people always bring that up?" Megan asked. "I fail to see the humor in an affair."

"It happened before we got here. Maybe if we'd lived here then, we'd find it funny too."

Megan sighed and handed Nancy back her phone. "You and Mary Beth are friends," she said. "Can't you get her to stop this nonsense?"

"Oh, I would imagine if you're dating someone, she'll stop," Nancy said.

"You think so?" she asked hopefully.

"Of course, one dinner date is not exactly going steady," Nancy reminded her. "Or do you have plans for another already?"

Megan wanted to lie and say yes, they did in fact have plans another date, but improvising wasn't her strong suit. She and Leah did *talk* about a second date though, but hadn't finalized a plan. Did that count?"

"Well?"

Megan nodded. "Yes...Leah mentioned getting together again," she said as casually as she could.

"Well, good for you," Nancy said with forced cheerfulness. "Maybe it'll work out this time."

"Like you said...it's not like we're going steady or anything."

CHAPTER NINETEEN

Leah stared at the picture once again, and once again she had to make herself stop as she laid her iPad face down. When she'd first seen it, she had nearly spit out her coffee. She imagined Megan was livid, but damn...what a nice way to bring in the morning. It didn't take much imagination to chase the shadow away from her left breast.

She smiled and shook her head. Yeah, Megan would be livid. She wondered if she'd seen it already. She took one more peek at it, her gaze traveling up the exposed leg and thigh, to the smooth curve of hip, past the trim waist, following the line of the sheet as it covered one breast, leaving the other exposed... and shadowed.

"Damn," she murmured.

Pounding on the outer door made her slam the iPad down guiltily, and she hurried from her office into the main room, finding Megan peering inside, her face cupped against the glass. She unlocked the door and opened it, silently inviting Megan into the shop.

"Have you seen it?" Megan demanded.

Leah thought it best to lie. "Seen what?"

Megan put her hands on her hips. "So you *haven't* seen it?"

Leah again feigned ignorance. "No. I don't think so. What are you talking about?"

Apparently—even though they didn't really know each other that well—Megan could see through the deception. She arched an eyebrow, pinning Leah to the spot with just that simple gesture.

And this time, Leah could no longer hide her smile. "Are you talking about Facebook?" she asked innocently.

Megan slugged her in the arm. "I *knew* you'd seen it! Can you *believe* she did that?"

"No! I'm shocked!"

Megan glared at her. "You could at least pretend to have some sympathy for me. A *real* girlfriend would be very upset that my picture is out there."

"You're right. Especially since *I* haven't seen you naked yet," Leah said with a smile. "And Mary Beth has."

"Oh...*God*," Megan groaned. "I can't believe this is happening to me."

"In all fairness...it's a very nice picture."

Megan sighed. "I'm too angry at Mary Beth to even pretend to be mad at you." She ran a hand through her hair. "We have a breakfast date tomorrow morning, by the way. There's a café near Susie's grocery store—Jay's Nest."

"Jay's Nest? Like...blue jay, the bird?"

"Play on words. Jay Bannister owns it," Megan explained. "But it's *the* breakfast place for the locals. Mary Beth and Sarah have a standing breakfast date every Wednesday." She paused. "You can go, right?"

She nodded with a shrug. "Sure. Mary Beth will be there?" She smiled. "This ought to be fun."

"Thank you." Megan turned to leave, then stopped. "And what was that...that *kiss* last night? Kissing was not a part of the plan."

"I wouldn't exactly call that a kiss," Leah said.

"Then what would you call it?"

Leah met her gaze, trying to decide if Megan's annoyance was directed at her or if it was still the result of Mary Beth's latest post. She decided the latter and gave her a teasing smile.

"I guess technically some would call it a first-date good night kiss," she said. "I think the first long kiss is after the second date. That would be the first real kiss. Which is why I wouldn't really call last night's thing a kiss."

Megan stared at her. "There will be no kissing. Ever."

"Well, yeah, it's not like it's real kissing, Megan. I mean, we're fake dating so it would only be fake kissing," she said reasonably. "You know, it's not like I want to kiss you."

Megan continued to stare at her. She finally nodded. "Okay. As weird as this whole situation is, I guess that makes sense." She turned to go, then stopped once again. "I'll pick you up at eight."

"And I will look forward to it."

"And don't look at my picture," Megan said. "Erase it from your mind."

"Of course," Leah said. "I barely glanced at it anyway."

"Uh-huh."

As soon as the door closed behind Megan, Leah let out a laugh. For some reason, she found Megan Phenix extremely adorable in her exasperated state. Her smile lingered as she went back into her office, her gaze landing on the iPad. She reached for it, then stopped. Surely she could find something else to entertain her this morning other than a shadowy, almost naked picture of Megan.

She sat down at her desk and pulled her laptop in front of her instead, going back to the emails she had only glanced through earlier. The large outdoor sign was going up tomorrow, and the displays and new shelving should be completed by Friday. Next week her inventory would start trickling in. She was both excited and apprehensive about that. She would soon open Ruby's for real. But what if she had no customers? She'd done enough research to know that the first month could be brutal for a new shop. A lot of the tourists who came to Eureka Springs were frequent visitors and not first-timers. And repeat visitors tended to go to familiar shops and restaurants, not new ones. She had to hope that because the Phenix Grill was the most popular eating place in town, Ruby's would get some exposure from people walking by on their way to eat. That was one advantage of having limited parking in town...a lot of customers simply walked the streets.

She sighed. No sense worrying about that now. She would have all summer.

CHAPTER TWENTY

Megan glanced around as inconspicuously as possible, feeling all eyes on them. Leah was perusing the menu, seemingly oblivious to the stares.

"This is too stressful," Megan whispered. "I feel like we're being scrutinized."

"I'm sure we are," Leah said easily. "How are the omelets?"

"The Mexican omelet is very good," she said as she picked up her coffee cup and took a sip. "I'm sure it falls into the Tex-Mex category though. Maybe you should avoid it."

Leah smiled. "It's got avocado. I think that's more California than Texas."

Megan stared at her. "You are a snob, aren't you."

Leah laughed quietly. "Only about wine and Mexican food."

The conversations going on around them stopped when the door opened and Megan swore she could have heard a pin drop. Mary Beth Sturgeon walked inside, and Megan's eyes darted back to Leah. "Oh, my God," she murmured as she touched a hand to her chest. "I'm going to hyperventilate."

Leah smiled reassuringly at her. "Everything's fine," she whispered.

"She's going to know we're faking," she said, her mouth barely moving as she spoke.

"Relax," Leah said, her eyes never leaving Megan's. "Look at me. Smile."

Mary Beth brushed past their table with barely a glance at them, and everyone in the room seemed to exhale at the same time, including Megan. She looked to her right, noting that Mary Beth had a perfect view of their table.

"I don't think I can eat anything," she whispered. "I'm so nervous, I'm likely to throw up."

"Why are you letting her get to you like this?"

"Because she has naked pictures of me!" she snapped as quietly as she could.

"And whose fault is that?" Leah asked with a teasing smile.

Megan wanted to knock the smile from her face but thought that would be a dead giveaway that they weren't really dating. Or maybe everyone would think they were having a lover's spat on only their second date. Instead of reaching across the table to strangle Leah, she forced a smile to her own face.

"It is, of course, my fault. And whoever brought the Patrón tequila," she added.

"You never did tell me the whole story," Leah said.

Megan sighed. She might as well get it over with. If Leah didn't hear it from her, no doubt she would eventually hear it from someone in town. "Erin—the Wicked Witch—called me. Nancy wouldn't let me answer my phone, but I did listen to her voice mail. It was a rambling message telling me how happy she was and what a wonderful year she'd had and blah, blah, blah," she said, echoing Nancy's description of the voice mail. "I was feeling sorry for myself," she admitted. "And lonely. And I was at a stupid surprise party that I wished Nancy hadn't thrown for me." She sighed again. "So I kidnapped the Patrón bottle and had my way with it."

"I thought you weren't really emotionally attached to her—Erin."

"I wasn't. She was ten years younger than me. We had no business dating in the first place."

"But she was cute," Leah supplied.

"Yes. And well…it *had* been eight years," she said pointedly.

Leah grinned. "So the sex was great, huh?"

"After eight years, a blow-up doll would have been great."

Leah laughed loudly, causing curious stares to be directed at them. Megan laughed too, then sobered when she saw Mary Beth watching them.

"Anyway, that's not the point," she continued. "It's just the fact that she cheated on me and then made a big production about it at my birthday, so the whole damn town knew."

"But you didn't date long, right?"

Megan shook her head. "No, only about six months or so. But I was very upfront with her at the start. I told her about Tammi. She knew that she'd cheated on me for nearly the whole four years we were together," she said. "She knew how I felt about that. I told her at the beginning…if we were going to date, then we were *only* going to date. I told her if she wasn't ready for that then she shouldn't commit to it."

"But she did commit."

"Yes. And I knew right away that it was a mistake on my part. I knew it wasn't going anywhere, I knew I wasn't going to fall in love with her. That's what makes me so angry," she said. "I should have ended things with her. Instead, we kept dating."

"And she cheated on you," Leah finished for her. "What about Tammi? Were you in love with her?"

"Yes. She was attractive. Charming. Funny." She smiled. "Nancy likes to add 'conniving.'" She paused when Bonnie returned to their table with a decanter of coffee in her hand.

"Decide what you want yet?" Bonnie asked.

She nodded. "I'll have the Mexican omelet," she said. "No avocado for me."

"I'll have the same," Leah said. "You can toss her avocado on mine," she added with a smile. "And I'd prefer Monterey Jack, if you have it."

"Sure thing." Bonnie touched Megan's shoulder and winked. "She's cute," she said, loud enough for Leah to hear.

Megan met Leah's gaze across the table, noting she had a slightly embarrassed look on her face. She looked back at Bonnie and smiled. "Yes, she is." As soon as Bonnie left, she asked, "Does that make you uncomfortable?"

"What? A compliment?"

"Being called cute."

"I'm too old to be called cute," Leah said.

Megan waved her protest away. "You're attractive and you know it."

"Well, thank you for thinking so," Leah said. "I'll admit, when I first stopped coloring my hair, I was very self-conscious about it."

"When did you go gray?"

"I was in my early twenties when my first gray hair popped up. By my late twenties, I was coloring it. My natural color is dark brown, but I kept it a little lighter than that," she said.

"But you gave up the fight?"

Leah smiled and nodded. "I was forty-four, and my parents and I had a three-week trip planned to Europe. I was so busy trying to tie up things at work and get packed and everything that I missed my hair appointment," she said. "I wore my hair a little longer back then and the gray was showing, but I couldn't squeeze in the time to get it colored. So I thought I'd just go with it and get it done when I got back."

Megan smiled. "What happened? Did you just say screw it?"

"Pretty much. By the time we got back, I had two inches of gray roots showing. I guess I hadn't realized just how gray I was. Instead of getting it colored, I got it cut very short, taking most of the brown off." She shrugged. "I let it grow out, got rid of the brown and here we are," she said, pointing to her head.

Megan's gaze swept over her, liking the style that Leah sported now. Parted on the side, her bangs were just long enough to brush her eyebrows. As if uncomfortable with her staring, Leah tucked a few strands behind her ear, revealing a twinkling diamond earring.

"I like your hair," Megan said truthfully. "And if you're wondering if it makes you look old, it doesn't. In fact, you look much younger than Nancy, but don't you dare tell her I said that."

"My age doesn't bother me," Leah said. "It's just a number. In the grand scheme of things, it's all about how you feel. I walk or use my bike for transportation as much as I can," she said. "I try to eat healthfully." Then she smiled. "Although since I've been here, I can't really say that's been going as planned."

"It's impossible to eat healthy if you eat out. I know. I own a restaurant," she said. "You don't even want to know how many calories and fat grams are in one of our burgers. Of course, that's why they're so good!"

Leah nodded. "I've flirted with being vegetarian, vegan even," she said. "On and off for the last thirty years. But I miss having a good steak every once in a while. And burgers." She smiled. "And cheese. Although of everything, dairy was the easiest to give up."

"I was a vegetarian in college," Megan said. "Three years."

"Why'd you stop?"

"A barbecue and beer party during football season was my undoing."

"You know, you never said where you're from."

"St. Louis," Megan said. "Our parents still live there. And barbecue was the hardest for me to give up. Smoked ribs," she said with a moan. "My dad makes the best ribs. He slow smokes them for hours and hours. Spicy enough to have a bite but not overly so and tender enough that the meat practically falls off the bone." She nearly licked her lips at the memory of her father's ribs. "He makes his own sauce too. A recipe he refuses to share with us."

"I'm not much for barbecue," Leah said.

"I guess not," she said. "You're from California, after all."

"I'll admit, we are grillers and not barbecuers," Leah said. "I am partial to grilled fish, by the way. In case, you know, you want to surprise me with dinner sometime."

Megan smiled. "I think if I surprise you with dinner, I'll have Johnny grill—"

She stopped when the door opened, seeing Sarah hurrying inside. Her hair was pulled back into its normal ponytail, and she paused to run a hand over it before heading to Mary Beth's table. Megan had been so comfortable chatting with Leah that she'd almost forgotten about Mary Beth and Sarah's standing breakfast date. And really, that was the only reason she was here with Leah in the first place—to let Mary Beth know that they were dating.

She leaned forward, keeping her voice low. "That was Sarah."

Leah nodded. "They're whispering." Then she smiled. "Much like we are."

Megan nearly laughed and leaned back. "I'm afraid to look over there. Does Mary Beth looked pissed?"

"She has shot daggers at me with her eyes, yes," Leah said. Then she looked past Megan and smiled, her eyes widening. "Good. Breakfast. I'm starving."

Bonnie placed two plates on the table, one covered with avocado slices and the other bare. The omelet shared the plate with fried potatoes and a somewhat wilted sprig of parsley. A bowl of salsa was placed in the middle of the table for them to share.

"Looks great," Leah said. "Thank you."

"My pleasure. Need more coffee?"

Leah shook her head. "None for me."

"I'm good," Megan said. "Thanks."

Leah dug into her omelet with gusto, moaning at the first bite. She then scooped up a spoonful of salsa and added that on top of the avocado.

"I take it you approve?"

"Excellent," Leah said. "But if I come here again, I'll order extra peppers and ask to have the avocado inside with the vegetables." She raised her eyebrow. "I take it you don't like avocados?"

"I don't like them with eggs," Megan corrected. "On a burger, I love them. And spicy, chunky guacamole is a favorite. In fact, Johnny makes great guacamole. It might even satisfy your superior California taste buds," she teased.

Leah smiled. "Well, at least you recognize that we are superior when it comes to Mexican food."

"You'll be singing a different tune when I drag you to El Gallo's for Tex-Mex," she said. "You're going to love their saucy, cheesy enchiladas so much, you'll be begging me to take you back there."

Leah gave her a flirty grin. "I may be begging you for something, but I doubt it'll be Tex-Mex."

CHAPTER TWENTY-ONE

Megan tapped her foot to the music as she filled a frosty mug with beer. It wasn't even six yet, but the place was hopping. It had been a gloriously warm and sunny day, with the weekend forecasted to be the same. Apparently the good weather was bringing tourists with it as she only recognized a few familiar faces sitting around the bar.

"It's almost like a Friday night in June, isn't it?" Nancy asked.

"I was just thinking that we were a little busier than last week," she said as she slid the beer down the bar to Ray, one of the locals who came almost every Friday. "Are you helping with tables?" she asked Nancy.

"No. Eileen said they were covered. I just came from the kitchen."

Megan nodded. While Nancy enjoyed helping with the food prep, she did not. She'd much rather help Clint at the bar than chop onions and slice tomatoes and the like.

"You ever going to tell me about your date with Leah?"

Megan had been intentionally quiet about it, wondering how long it would be before Nancy quizzed her. So she shrugged. "It was breakfast. Not much to tell," she said truthfully. "Although Mary Beth was there."

"Yes, I heard."

"Oh?"

"She and Sarah have breakfast there every Wednesday," Nancy said. "I thought you knew that."

"I assure you, I do not keep up with Mary Beth's breakfast schedule," she lied. Then, "Why? What did she say?"

"She said she was glad she saw you."

Megan frowned. "Why's that?"

"She said it eased her fears," Nancy said.

"What fears?" she asked, her voice sounding a bit nervous to her own ears.

"Her fear that you and Leah were already romantically involved. She said she didn't see anything to indicate that you were more than friends."

Megan scoffed. "It was our second date. And really, it was breakfast. Can you even call that a date?"

"Well…was it a date?"

Oh…damn. What the hell did they need to do for people to think they were dating? Have sex on the table or something? But she would play innocent.

"Well, there was no sloppy kiss afterward, if that's what you mean."

"So are you dating or not?"

Megan threw up her hands. "We went out to dinner. We went out for breakfast. What constitutes dating? We're not having sex, if that's what you're asking," she said bluntly. "And I've not seen her since Wednesday morning." She groaned silently. Good Lord, was she trying to convince Nancy that they *weren't* dating?

"So you're not really interested in her?"

"I like her fine," she said. "We're getting to know each other."

"So you are interested in her?"

"Interested in dating? Interested in a relationship? Interested in...*what*?"

It was Nancy's turn to throw up her hands. "You're being difficult!"

"You're asking too many questions!"

"Do you like her or not? That's a simple question."

"We've managed to get through two meals without too much arguing. I like her better now than when I first met her. How's that?"

"Again...you're being difficult," Nancy said as she huffed off.

"Need two 'ritas on the rocks," Eileen called from the other side of the bar. "Top shelf, no salt on one."

Megan was glad for the interruption, and she went about mindlessly squeezing lime juice into the cocktail shaker. God, what was with Nancy and all the questions? She sighed. Maybe she should invite Leah over to the bar. She could sit at the end, and they could pretend to visit during slow times. But she looked around. It was a Friday night. There would be no slow times.

"Hey, you."

She turned at the sound of the familiar voice, an involuntary smile on her face. "I was just thinking about you."

"Oh, yeah? Does that mean I'm growing on you?" Leah asked with a smile.

"I just got grilled by Nancy regarding our status," she said quietly as she added tequila and Grand Marnier to the shaker. "Apparently, Mary Beth has decided that there's nothing romantic going on between us."

"Told you," Leah said. "We need to have some fake kissing or something."

"It should not be this stressful. Or this complicated," she said as she filled the margarita glasses. "Hang on." She took the drinks over to Eileen, then grabbed an empty beer mug from the bar. "Another?" she asked the young man who nodded without stopping his conversation with his companion.

"What we should do is this," Leah said. "After closing, you should come over to my place instead of going home. Hang out for an hour or so."

"Even though we stop serving food at nine, the bar stays open until ten. By the time we close and get out of here tonight, it'll be eleven, at least." She crossed the bar and set the fresh beer down. "If I go to your place, I'll fall asleep on the sofa."

"That's okay too," Leah said. "No one will know. I'll even let you park right in front of the store."

Megan grinned. "Finally! Parking is the only reason I'm going out with you, you know."

"I figured as much."

Megan nodded. "Okay. I guess going to your apartment is as good as we're going to get right now." She leaned closer. "I *told* you this whole thing was a bad idea."

Leah smiled. "Why do you keep forgetting that this was your idea?"

"No, no, no. *You* brought it up to begin with." She pulled a cold mug from the freezer. "You want a beer?"

Leah nodded. "Yes, please. And a good girlfriend would offer dinner too."

Megan laughed teasingly. "What makes you think I'm a good girlfriend?" Then her smile faded. "But I guess I'm really not. Maybe that's why I get cheated on."

Leah's smile faded too. "Megan, people who cheat on their partners don't need a reason. That's just what they do…they're serial cheaters. Maybe it's some sort of a thrill for them to see if they can get away with it." She smiled again. "Normal people— if you're a bad girlfriend—would simply break up with you and go on about their business."

Megan sighed. "I suppose. But when this is over with, can I please be the one to break up with you?"

"Of course. Just as long as you don't announce you're switching to men."

"Oh…*gross*," Megan said with an exaggerated shudder, causing Leah to laugh.

* * *

Leah had to admit that she was enjoying this little game she and Megan were playing. When she'd first mentioned it, it had seemed like the perfect solution. She was new in town and she was single—she had no desire to be chased by every available woman in the county. Megan's situation was a little more dismal. At least Leah didn't have a crazy woman stalking her. But still, she tended to agree with Megan when she doubted that they'd be able to pull it off. The main reason being…they didn't really like each other. She'd perceived Megan as grumpy and argumentative, and Megan had perceived her as arrogant and annoying. And a bully, because she took away her parking spot.

But now? Now she found Megan's slight grumpiness endearing. And arguing was kinda fun. And she hoped Megan no longer thought of her as arrogant and annoying, two words she would have never used to describe herself. As shocking as it was—especially considering how things started out with them—she felt like they were becoming friends. When she left California, she left behind a handful of good friends but none that she would consider close friends or best friends. One of her goals when she moved here was to try to build some meaningful relationships. Of the few locals she'd met so far, Nancy and Megan Phenix were the only two she could envision becoming good friends with, even though Nancy was still a little cool to her.

She slid her gaze over to Megan, lingering on her face as she slept. Megan was on her side, curled into the corner of the leather sofa, a throw pillow under her cheek, her hands tucked under her chin. Her lips were parted slightly, her eyelids fluttering as she dreamed. True to her word, Megan had settled on the sofa as soon as she got there, accepting a bottle of water from Leah. They'd talked only a little before Megan's yawns became more pronounced. Leah had turned the TV on, telling Megan to get comfortable. Five minutes later, she was asleep.

As she watched Megan sleep, she couldn't help but think about the pictures that Mary Beth had posted. It didn't take much imagination for her to recall every smooth curve that Mary Beth had revealed. She pulled her eyes away guiltily, glancing back toward the TV. It was an old *Seinfeld* rerun that she'd seen a dozen times already so she turned the sound down even further, letting her gaze slowly drift back to Megan.

CHAPTER TWENTY-TWO

Megan yawned as she watched coffee drip into her cup. Nancy was leaning against the counter, sipping her own.

"So what time did you get home last night?"

"It was...late," she said vaguely.

Actually, it was barely after one when she'd crept silently into the house, but she would let Nancy think what she would. When Leah had awakened her, she'd been sleeping so soundly, she could barely open her eyes. But finding those smoky gray ones looking back at her had startled her so badly, she'd nearly jumped off the sofa.

"Late like two or three? Or what?"

Megan paused to add sugar to her coffee, trying to decide if she should lie or not. After all, this was her sister. Yes, her sister who was friends with Mary Beth Sturgeon. She should lie. But then Nancy would assume that since she'd stayed that long at Leah's apartment, they had most certainly entertained themselves in a more intimate fashion than watching TV. Was she ready to answer questions like that? She sighed.

"It wasn't quite that late," she conceded.

Nancy's smile was teasing. "So? Are you going to give me details?"

"Details?"

"Well, you're not glowing, so I'll assume you didn't have sex."

"Oh, my God! I've had two dates with her. I barely know her. Why in the world would I sleep with her?"

"Umm…because she's cute, for one. And two, you're getting older and grumpier by the minute. Sex would do you good."

"Okay…for one, I am *not* grumpy. And two…the last time you suggested sex would do me good, I ended up with Erin." She glared at her. "And I think your reasoning was the same— she was cute."

"Erin was cute, but practically a child. Leah is a mature, attractive woman who apparently likes you for some crazy reason. My advice to you…don't screw this one up."

Nancy was being serious and very sweet, and Megan felt a twinge of guilt for lying to her. But only a twinge. And as soon as this mess with Mary Beth was over with, she'd come clean. But in the meantime…

"Well, I'll be mindful of your advice," she said. "But as far as sex…we're not there yet."

Nancy seemed to study her for a moment, then she pushed off the counter.

"I should shower. I'm going by Susie's this morning," she said. "I'm about out of coffee and I'm down to my last muffin for breakfast."

Megan nodded. "Okay. I'm going to hit the treadmill."

Which was the last thing she felt like doing this morning. Six hours of sleep had left her feeling sluggish, but she knew a run would make her feel better. And after that, maybe she'd take time for a real breakfast as her stomach reminded her that the turkey sandwich she'd shared with Nancy last night wasn't enough to be considered dinner.

She was slipping on her running shoes when her phone rang. It was a California number, and she assumed it was a telemarketer. She was about to end the call, then remembered she had given Leah her number.

"Hello," she said.

"Hey...I wanted to make sure you didn't oversleep. You were a little out of it when I woke you."

Megan smiled. "Thank you. Actually, I was about to hit the treadmill." She glanced around her, making sure Nancy wasn't near. "And I should apologize for falling asleep on you, but it was a busy night."

"Well, you did warn me in advance," Leah said. "Enjoy your run. I'll talk to you later."

She was gone before Megan could say more, and she sighed, wondering at the budding friendship between them. Considering how rude she'd been when they first met—and yes, she would admit that she had been a tad snarky to Leah—she was surprised at how easily Leah seemed to forget that. Megan had been neither nice nor friendly to her, yet Leah was being both of those things now.

Megan sighed again, trying to remind herself that she wasn't even sure if she liked Leah. They might be on friendly terms now, but she was still the arrogant, parking-space hoarder she'd been when they met.

She turned on the treadmill and started out slow to warm up, her thoughts still on Leah. Maybe arrogant was too strong a word. Leah was simply confident, sure of herself. No need to call her arrogant. A hoarder of parking spaces? Megan smiled and nodded. Yeah, she was still that.

CHAPTER TWENTY-THREE

Megan had just finished writing out the day's lunch special on the board—meatloaf and mashed potatoes—when the door opened. She turned, smiling automatically in greeting. Her smile faltered, however, as Mary Beth Sturgeon stood there. Megan looked around frantically, hoping Nancy was near, but she was apparently still in the kitchen. So instead of running and hiding—which is what she wanted to do—Megan squared her shoulders and nodded curtly at her.

"Mary Beth. Table for one?"

A grin that would rival that of the Cheshire Cat lit Mary Beth's face. "Hello, my angel," she said, her raspy voice echoing in the lobby.

Megan squeezed her eyes shut for a few seconds. *God!* When she opened them, Mary Beth was still there, still grinning. She had something up her sleeve, Megan could tell. She apparently wasn't there for lunch.

"Is there something…I can help you with?" she choked out.

"Now that is a loaded question."

Megan refused to return her smile. "The lunch crowd will be here soon. Or would you like a table?" she tried again.

Mary Beth walked closer. "I'd like to chat, if you have a moment."

Megan shook her head. "I'm really, really busy," she said. "Really busy."

Mary Beth looked around slowly, then brought her gaze back to Megan. There were only three other people in the grill. Megan sighed.

"Fine. What do you want?" she asked bluntly.

"I wanted to discuss your…well, your social life."

Megan narrowed her eyes. "My social life is none of your business."

"I beg to differ."

Megan balled her hands into fists, afraid she might smack the grin right off Mary Beth's face.

"What is it you want to know?"

"You and this Leah person…what exactly is happening here?"

Megan was suddenly very nervous as Mary Beth's eyes bored into hers. "What do you mean?"

"Well, some say you're dating." Mary Beth shook her head. "I, for one, don't believe it."

"Of course we're dating. Why would you think we're not?"

"For starters, I can't see you with someone that old," Mary Beth said.

Megan laughed. "You do realize that she is younger than you are, right?"

Mary Beth looked shocked. "She's totally gray! At least I have the good sense to color my hair so I don't look like I'm in my fifties!"

Megan's gaze traveled over Mary Beth, taking in her slightly plump figure and her conservative clothes, noting that her shoulder-length light brown hair could stand to be clipped. Leah looked at least ten years younger than Mary Beth. Her short, stylish hair and trim, athletic body gave her a youthful appearance. Of course, she wasn't about to share her thoughts with Mary Beth.

"Anyway, after seeing you at breakfast last week, well, I wouldn't consider you two dating. I just don't see it."

"I don't know what you mean."

"I've heard a rumor that you might be faking this. That your nighttime trips to her apartment are, well, let's just say… platonic."

Megan gasped in mock surprise, pretending to be offended. "Like…like we're *fake* dating? *Really?* You think I would stoop that low?"

Mary Beth gave her a sly grin. "If I find out you're doing this just to try to throw me off your trail, there will be no mercy."

Megan stared at her. "Throw you off my *trail?* I wasn't aware I had a trail." She put her hands on her hips. "And are you threatening me? *Really?* You already have pictures of me on your Facebook page. What else can you possibly do?"

The sly grin turned smug as Mary Beth pulled out her phone. Megan watched as she flipped through several images before stopping. She held the phone up for Megan to see.

Megan shrieked as her eyes widened. "Oh. My. Freakin'. *God.*" She pulled her gaze from the phone and glared at Mary Beth. "Youhaveanakedpictureofmeonyourphone!" she said in a rush, her voice two octaves higher than normal. She pulled Mary Beth to the side. "*Why* do you have a naked picture of me on your phone? Jesus…who all have you shown this to?" she demanded.

"I haven't shown this to anyone," Mary Beth said. "What happens in my bed, stays in my bed."

Megan was shocked speechless for several seconds before she found her voice. "Nothing *happened* in your bed!" she snapped.

Mary Beth touched her arm. "But we were so close, angel. So close."

Megan held her hands up. "Stop. Just…just stop. You're making me crazy."

"Yes," Mary Beth drawled. "I've been told I do that to women."

Oh, God, Megan groaned silently.

"Anyway," Mary Beth said as she put her phone up. "I'm having a dinner party Tuesday evening. Nancy has already accepted. Julie and Sarah will be there too. I expect you and this Leah person to be there as well." She took a step closer. "I'll have my eyes on you."

Megan shook her head. "Really…Nancy and I shouldn't both be gone from the grill at the same time. Maybe—"

"Nancy already said it would be fine. Tuesdays are slow, she said."

Megan tried to smile through her gritted teeth. "Of course she did," she managed.

Mary Beth took another step closer, and Megan took one back. "You know, angel, I could cancel the whole thing and you and I could have a nice, quiet dinner…just the two of us. What do you say?"

"I am *not* going on a date with you. Besides…I'm dating Leah now."

Mary Beth laughed quietly. "So you say." She mercifully stepped away from her finally. "Well, I'll see you Tuesday."

"Look forward to it," she lied with a smile on her face.

As soon as Mary Beth left, she spun on her heels and headed straight for the kitchen. Nancy was nowhere in sight.

"She went to the office," Johnny said as he opened the oven door, revealing several pans of meatloaf.

"Smells great," she said. "Need help with anything?" she asked, knowing he would say no.

"We got it."

She nodded, then headed for the office, taking time to make sure there wasn't anyone waiting to be seated. She had hostess duty until Pam arrived at two. She found Nancy at the window, guiltily shoving her phone into her pocket. Megan looked at her expectantly, raising both eyebrows.

"What?" Nancy asked as she sat down behind the desk.

"What are you up to?"

"I don't know what you're talking about," Nancy said as she pulled the laptop in front of her.

Megan put her hands on her hips. "Couldn't warn me?"

"About what?"

"You know very well what I mean," she said. "Mary Beth was just here."

"Oh. You mean her dinner party."

Megan narrowed her eyes. "If I didn't know better, I'd think you were in cahoots with her."

"Cahoots?" Nancy laughed. "Who says cahoots?"

Megan waved her hand in the air. "You know what I mean. What's going on?"

"Nothing's going on. She's having a dinner party."

"A dinner party that includes Sarah and Julie, the two other women—besides Mary Beth—who have asked me out the most. I hardly think that's a coincidence, do you?"

"As usual, you're reading too much into it."

"Mary Beth insinuated that there are some people who don't think Leah and I are really dating," she said. "Wonder where she would have heard that from?"

"Are you accusing me?"

Megan blew out her breath and ran a hand through her hair. "I don't know. I only know she's driving me insane. She has a naked picture of me on her phone, for Christ's sake!"

Nancy's eyes widened. "Really? How naked?"

"Naked naked! She's *crazy*!"

"Oh, Megan, she's not crazy. She's just—"

"Do I have to do everything around here?" Eileen said at the door. "It *is* lunchtime, you know."

"Oh, God...I'm hostess today," Megan said. "Sorry." She turned to leave, then looked back at Nancy. "We're not through."

"Whatever," Nancy said as she waved her away.

CHAPTER TWENTY-FOUR

Leah held up the chimes, her eyes watching as the sunlight bounced off the shiny aluminum tubes. As she'd done with the others, she lightly brushed the windcatcher, setting the chimes in motion. Their metallic tones were deeper, more earthy than the others. Instead of hanging it on the rack with the dozen or so she'd already unpacked, she set this one aside, thinking she would hang it near the door and let the breeze do its magic. During spring and fall, she envisioned leaving the front door open as she'd seen other shop owners do. It was much more inviting for customers than being met with a closed door, especially in a new, unknown shop such as hers.

She stood back and looked around. Her little shop was slowly filling up with merchandise. Soon she would be ready to open for business. The sign was up out front, the displays and shelves were all in place, and the inventory was coming in faster than she could catalog it and get it put up. All that was left was hanging the sign in the door stating the hours and the big "OPEN" sign she'd ordered for the front window. Truth was, she could open right now. She had enough stuff. But the real truth was, she was scared to death to actually put the sign in the window.

Which was ridiculous. No matter what happened the first few months, the first summer, the first season, she had no plans other than to see it through. In fact, she'd planned to give herself three years to make it work, tweaking the inventory as needed until she hit on the right combination.

"So quit worrying about it," she murmured as she opened up yet another box.

This one was filled with greeting cards. She'd debated between funny cards and environmental cards. She held up the mountain scene, the trees shrouded in fog. Environmental cards with inspirational messages won out. She was stocking the card rack when the front door burst open. She turned, finding Megan standing there with a panicked look on her face.

"What's wrong?"

"You won't believe what—" But she stopped, pausing to look around, her expression changing to one of surprise. "Oh, my God! You've got stuff in here."

Leah smiled. "You're not a very attentive girlfriend, are you? I told you the inventory was coming in this week."

"Oh, yeah, you did. I'm sorry," Megan said, waving her hand in the air. "I have too much stress in my life to keep up with my fake girlfriend's goings-on."

"Well, you'll be happy to know that I'll be opening very, very soon so all those parking spaces won't go to waste any longer," she teased. "That is, if I have any customers."

"Are you worried?"

"Of course. It's not like I know what I'm doing."

Megan walked over to the rack of chimes and put them in motion, the store filling with musical tones. Then she walked over to the large bin which was stuffed with T-shirts. Leah had only begun hanging them up on the wall to display them.

"You can't go wrong with T-shirts," Megan said. "Take your lowest cost T-shirts and, instead of mixing them in with the others, have them on a sale rack. Customers will then think they're getting a deal on the price. Or have a special every day or every week featuring a couple of shirts that are on sale."

Leah nodded. "Good ideas. Thanks." She leaned against one of the empty tables. "Now, what's wrong?"

Megan sighed. "We have a problem."

Leah frowned. "What kind of a problem?"

"Mary Beth suspects this isn't real," Megan said, motioning between the two of them.

"What? Us dating?"

"Yes. She thinks I'm faking it," Megan said. "And she's lost her freakin' mind. She showed me a picture on her phone. A picture of me. A *naked* picture of me."

Leah laughed. "Can it get any more naked than what she's posted?"

"Yes! I mean, totally naked. Like, the sheet is pulled off and I'm lying there..." Megan grabbed the bridge of her nose. "Oh, God...I will kill her if she posts that. I mean, *kill* her."

"Surely she wouldn't post it," Leah said. "That's going too far."

"She made a veiled threat. Meaning...if she finds out that I'm only faking this with you to throw her off my trail—her words, not mine—then she might be compelled to post the photo." Megan growled. "She's freakin' *insane*!"

"She won't post it, Megan. If I were her, I'd be worried about being banned from Facebook—or worse, a lawsuit—not worried whether you're really dating me or not."

Megan nodded. "You're right. I don't think she would actually post it. Just the fact that she's got it on her phone and she showed it to me makes me want to strangle her!" Megan said, holding her fingers in a circle, pretending to choke someone. "Anyway, she's having a dinner party Tuesday night. Julie, Sarah and Nancy will be there." She paused. "And you and me. You can go, right?"

Leah nodded. "Sure. I take it we're to be on display?"

Megan slowly shook her head. "Should it be this complicated to pretend to date?"

"It'll be fine," she said. "We'll be fine. We'll go together. As a couple. They'll all be convinced and this will all be over with before you know it."

Megan sighed. "I'm beginning to think that the only way they'll be convinced is if we have sex on the dinner table."

Leah grinned. "Well...if you insist."

Megan laughed, the smile chasing some of the anxiety from her face. "I know I said kissing was against the rules, but I'd really like a big, sloppy kiss right in front of Mary Beth."

Leah was surprised at the jolt that visual gave her. "That could probably be arranged."

Megan nodded. "Well," she pointed out the door. "I should really get back."

"Busy today?"

"Yes. The weekends are picking up." Megan paused at the door. "If you feel like dinner, why don't you come over later? I'm working the bar tonight."

Leah nodded. "Okay. A burger sounds good."

Even though she knew the grill would be packed on a Saturday and she and Megan would have little time to visit, it beat staying here alone and eating a frozen burrito. Maybe she needed to start cooking again. Maybe she'd invite Megan over. They could have an early dinner one night before the regular dinner crowd showed up next door. She nodded to herself. Yeah...maybe next week she'd do that.

CHAPTER TWENTY-FIVE

Megan was nervous and she wasn't entirely sure why. It was simply a causal dinner party with friends. That's all it was. They could all suspect and conjure up what they wanted as far as she and Leah were concerned, but as long as they continued to go out and date, then that should be the end of it. She needed to quit worrying about it. What was the worst that could happen? So Mary Beth put a naked picture of her out there? So what? It wouldn't be the end of the world. Well…it might be for Mary Beth. She allowed herself a small smile as she pictured herself strangling Mary Beth with her bare hands. Of course, she wasn't sure how good she'd look in an orange jumpsuit as they hauled her away to prison.

She shook that image away. No. Mary Beth wouldn't dare post the picture. Even if she found out that she and Leah weren't really dating—and there was no way she could find out as long as she and Leah stuck to the story—she doubted Mary Beth would go through with it. Even *she* wouldn't stoop that low.

"All set?"

Megan nodded. "I suppose."

"It'll be fine. Don't worry."

Leah was dressed in jeans, as was she. She'd taken her break at three to go home and shower and change. Nancy had left at five, saying she would meet them at Mary Beth's as she'd promised to help cook. Nancy had been a little secretive about it, and Megan again wondered what they were up to. Surely to God Nancy wasn't helping Mary Beth in this little sick game of hers.

"Call me if you need something," she said to Eileen as they left.

"I'll try not to burn the place down. Go have fun."

"Fun, she says," Megan murmured.

It was a pleasant evening and Leah had suggested they walk the few blocks up the hill to Mary Beth's house. While she had nothing against walking—and sure, walking was practical and good for you—it just wasn't something she did. In fact, it wasn't something any of them did. At least, not on a regular basis. It was so ingrained in everyone to hop in their car and go where they needed to go, she doubted walking ever crossed their minds. But it did give her a chance to relax. Or at least *try* to relax.

"You're being awfully quiet."

"I'm nervous," she admitted.

Leah surprised her by taking her hand. Megan's fingers entwined with hers, and their hands swung casually between them as they walked.

"You know, not a single person has asked me out since you and I had dinner that first night," Leah said. "Before we went out, I had at least six or eight dinner invitations."

"Well, I'm glad this arrangement is working out for you," she said dryly.

"Hopefully, after tonight, Mary Beth will leave you alone," Leah said. She raised her eyebrows teasingly. "You know, wet, sloppy fake kisses and all that."

Megan had really been teasing when she'd mentioned them kissing. Apparently Leah had taken it to heart. Oh well, maybe a fake kiss or two would be enough to convince Mary Beth that there really was no chance for her. She had to mentally shake her head. She wasn't actually contemplating *kissing* Leah Rollins, was she?

As they walked up the sidewalk toward Mary Beth's house, she felt her heart hammering in her chest. She wasn't sure if it was from being nervous or from the memory of the last time she'd been here.

"We should have practiced."

Leah raised an eyebrow. "Practiced what? Holding hands?" she asked as she raised their linked hands between them.

"Kissing," Megan said quietly.

A smile played on Leah's lips. "Well, we could practice now, if you'd like. I could probably be forced to, you know, if you insisted."

Megan arched an eyebrow. "This isn't fun and games, you know." She took a deep breath. "I'm nervous as hell." She squeezed Leah's fingers. "And if Mary Beth is cruel enough to have tequila here, please don't let me near the stuff."

Leah laughed. "Oh, that's right. This is the scene of the crime, isn't it? Do you think Mary Beth has been dreaming of that night?"

"She stripped me naked and posed me for pictures," Megan said. "Surely there's some kind of law against that."

"Did you ever threaten her with a lawsuit?"

"You can't do that. Not in a town this small. Everyone would take sides and I would lose."

"You're the victim."

"Everyone has the same thought on it as Nancy does—Mary Beth is just having a little fun." She waved her hand dismissively. "And if it was anyone else but me, I'd be enjoying the posts as much as the next person."

"Well, hopefully there won't be any more posts from her." Leah grinned. "Although I wouldn't be opposed to seeing the naked picture."

Before she could stop herself, Megan slugged Leah in the arm. "You are *so* bad. A good girlfriend would be demanding she delete it from her phone immediately."

Leah rubbed her arm and laughed. "Well, if it'll make you feel better, I'll demand to see it for myself to deem whether it should be deleted or not."

Megan wiggled a finger at her. "You're enjoying this way too much."

Leah led her up onto the porch, a smile still on her face. "I'll admit, yes, it's been a little fun."

Before she could knock, the door opened, and Mary Beth stood there staring at them, a predatory smile on her face.

"Having a spat, angel?"

Megan frowned. "No. Why?"

"I saw you hit her."

Megan laughed. "No, we were just playing around." She turned to Leah. "Why did I hit you again?"

"I believe it was because I was curious to see the naked photo." She looked at Mary Beth. "She tells me you have one of her on your phone."

The smile on Mary Beth's face never faltered. "Well, I guess that means you've not had the pleasure of seeing her in all her glory," she said with a wave at Megan's body. "Pity that I have and you haven't." Mary Beth looked pointedly at Megan. "What does that say, angel?"

"It says that I avoid tequila from now on."

Mary Beth laughed. "Oh, angel…we can reminisce about that night later." She finally stepped back. "Come in, come in," she offered. "Glad you could both make it." She surprised Megan by holding her hand out to Leah. "Nice to see you again, Leah."

Leah shook her hand. "Thanks. You too."

Mary Beth led them inside, and Leah gave Megan a subtle wink as she again took her hand. Megan grasped it, squeezing her fingers tightly, surprised at the confidence she felt just from Leah's touch.

"You know Nancy, of course," Mary Beth said, motioning to the recliner where Nancy was lounging. "This is Sarah and Julie," she introduced.

Leah nodded. Julie appeared to be even thinner than she remembered. "Yes. I met Julie at the kickoff party last month," she said. "Good to see you again."

She turned to Sarah, a woman who appeared to be a little younger than herself. Her brown hair—showing gray at the temples—was pulled back into a ponytail, giving her a youthful look.

She held her hand out. "Leah Rollins. Nice to meet you."

"You too," Sarah nodded, "I've heard a lot about you."

"Come sit by me," Julie said, her thin voice again matching her appearance. She patted the sofa beside her. "I'm dying to hear how you got Megan to go out with you."

"What would you like to drink?" Mary Beth asked. "I have beer, wine, water." She turned to Megan. "And I made a pitcher of margaritas. Patrón tequila. I know it's your favorite."

Megan barely controlled her urge to gag at the mention of Patrón tequila. "Wine, please."

"Leah?"

Megan saw the indecision on Leah's face and hid her smile when Leah opted for a beer instead of her beloved wine, no doubt not wanting to chance it being something other than California wine.

Nancy handed Megan her empty glass. "I'll take a margarita, please."

"Why don't you come with me?" Megan asked, her gaze following Mary Beth into the kitchen. Leah had already been pulled down beside Julie.

"She won't hurt you," Nancy said. "Besides, I want to hear how Leah got you to go out with her too."

Megan flicked her gaze to Leah, about to panic, when Leah smiled and launched into the story of when they first met.

"Then she stormed into my shop with my note wadded up in her fist. She had a fiery look in her eyes that captivated me from the start," Leah said, smiling at Megan. "I never knew anyone could be so passionate about parking spaces."

Megan tuned out their laughter as she sorted through the four bottles of wine—all red—surprised that two of the four were from California. She chose the zinfandel for herself. She swirled it in her glass for a second before tasting. It was rich and robust, and she imagined that Leah would like that much better than the beer Mary Beth had pulled out for her.

"Leah is partial to California wine," Megan explained. "I think I'll offer her a glass of this zinfandel."

"Do you like that? I prefer the sweeter white zinfandel myself." Mary Beth motioned to a fifth bottle that she'd just opened. "Julie is having the merlot. I've developed a taste for that as well." Mary Beth refilled Nancy's glass from the pitcher of margaritas. "I'll take this to Nancy."

Megan eyed her suspiciously. She was being too nice. Too normal. Something was obviously very wrong, she thought, as Mary Beth hurried from the kitchen. Megan followed, noting the smiles that everyone sported.

"After that first encounter, she called you annoying and irritating," Nancy said with a laugh, ignoring the glare Megan gave her.

"She also estimated my age at seventy-five," Leah added.

"I was teasing," Megan said in her defense. "Nancy was going on and on about how cute you were and she wanted to know how old I thought you were." She glanced at Nancy, glad to see a blush on her face. She handed Leah the glass of wine, nodding at her unasked question. Leah took a sip and smiled.

"Very good. Thank you."

Megan found herself relegated to the background as the others peppered Leah with questions. Of course, in all fairness, most of the questions were personal in nature. Where did Leah come from? Why Eureka Springs? When would her shop be open? How old was she really? And Megan's favorite…are you two going steady? But it was Sarah's question that nearly made her choke on her wine.

"Does it bother you that most of the town has seen her naked?"

To Leah's credit, she didn't seem thrown by the question at all.

"Naked in that she's an exhibitionist or naked in that someone is posting pictures of her against her will?"

It could be construed that Leah was teasing based on her smile, but Megan recognized her tone for what it was. Apparently Mary Beth did too as she gave a nervous laugh.

"I don't believe Megan's name was ever associated with the pictures."

"My hair and the side of my face is showing on a couple of them," Megan contradicted. "That's as good as a name."

"Oh, Megan," Julie laughed. "I can assure you no one is looking at your face."

"I never knew my sister had such nice legs," Nancy added.

"That's the truth," Sarah said, staring at Megan as if she could see through her jeans.

"Treadmill," Nancy continued. "I think I'm going to take it up."

Megan felt like she was in a dream, a very bad dream, as they talked around her as if she wasn't there. She locked eyes with Leah, her amused expression making Megan smile. A little. Very little.

Thankfully, the conversation drifted from her to the town, and everyone started sharing stories of tourists and who was busy and who wasn't. Sarah seemed the most interested in Leah's new shop. Julie, who sold chocolates and ice cream, didn't seem concerned with the competition, but Sarah was blatantly asking what Leah intended to sell and why.

"I don't think my little shop will cut into your sales," Leah said.

"But you do intend to sell windsocks and flags too?"

Leah shrugged. "I'll probably have a few but certainly nothing like what you carry, Sarah. I don't plan to specialize in any one thing."

"So you've been to my shop?"

Leah nodded. "Last summer I did some…some reconnaissance."

Mary Beth laughed. "She means snooping."

Leah laughed too. "Yeah, that too."

All in all, it was one of the most stressful evenings Megan had endured in quite some time. Nancy was watching them like a hawk, as was Mary Beth. Julie and Sarah were occupying Leah, giving her and Leah little to no time together. In fact, they'd not had a chance for even one private moment between them. On the outside looking in, she would have to agree that their relationship appeared to be only platonic, at best.

So when dinner was ready, she made it a point to sit beside Leah, beating Sarah to the chair by a fraction of a second. Julie had already claimed the one on the other side of Leah.

"You're popular this evening," she murmured.

Leah appeared to be unfazed by all the attention she was receiving, and she smiled quickly at Megan before turning to Julie, responding to a question she'd asked.

Megan blew out her breath in frustration, finding Nancy watching her. She raised her eyebrows questioningly, but Nancy only smiled and went to help Mary Beth in the kitchen. She blew out her breath again, impatiently tapping her foot, wishing the dinner was already over with.

"I hope everyone likes manicotti," Mary Beth said as she returned, bringing a huge platter to the table. Nancy followed with a large bowl of mixed salad. Garlic bread had already been passed around.

"That looks wonderful," Leah said. "Did you actually find all of the ingredients at Susie's store?"

Everyone laughed, even Megan.

"Of course not," Mary Beth said.

Leah looked at Megan questioningly. "I thought it was forbidden for the locals to use the supermarket down the hill."

"Oh, it is," Julie said.

"So?"

"We sneak out of town and go to the supermarket in Berryville," Sarah explained.

"I see. And does Susie know?"

"She pretends that she doesn't know," Nancy said. "And no one talks about it."

"So why not just use the one down the hill then?"

Mary Beth gasped. "Are you kidding? Someone might see us. Word would get back to Susie before we even made it back up the hill."

Megan patted Leah's thigh. "I'll explain later," she said with a smile.

Before she could remove her hand, Leah's own covered it, holding it there against her thigh. Megan nearly jerked it away before she remembered that they *were* supposed to be dating. Besides, Leah's hand was soft and warm and surprisingly, her touch seemed to bring some normalcy to the evening. She allowed her hand to rest there a few more seconds before gently pulling away.

* * *

"I'll check on things at the grill," Megan told Nancy. "No need for you to come down."

"Good. Because I think I had one too many margaritas," Nancy said as she slumped down into one corner of the sofa.

"Tequila and Mary Beth don't mix," Megan warned. "I hope we don't see *your* photo on her Facebook page tomorrow."

That statement sent Nancy into a fit of giggles, and Megan turned to Leah and shrugged. "Maybe I *do* hope it's her picture and not mine."

Leah laughed and took her arm. "Come on. Let's tell the others goodbye and get out of here."

She led Megan into the kitchen where Julie and Sarah were helping Mary Beth with a coffee tray. Leah was almost tempted to stay as the aroma of the freshly ground coffee made her long for a taste. However, she knew Megan was ready to leave.

"We're going to pass on coffee," she said.

"You're leaving already?" Sarah asked.

"I need to check in at the grill," Megan said. "Dinner was very good, Mary Beth. Thank you."

"I picked up a pie from Craig's. You sure you don't want to stay for dessert?"

"Better not," Megan said.

"Well, I'm glad you both came," Mary Beth said. "We should do it again."

Leah nodded. "Once I get my shop opened, maybe I'll have dinner at my apartment for everyone." She glanced at Sarah. "Give you a chance to see Ruby's."

"That sounds nice," Sarah said. "Look forward to it."

"Me too," Julie added.

Megan was already backing out of the room, and Leah smiled quickly at them. "See you later. Thanks again."

As soon as they were on the porch and the door closed, Megan turned to her. "Something's going on."

"What do you mean?"

"She was too nice."

"Mary Beth?"

"What do you think she's planning?"

Leah stepped off the porch and Megan followed. "Why do you think she's planning something?"

"Because she wasn't…she just wasn't right."

"I thought she was kinda pleasant."

"I *know*. That's what I mean. She's up to something."

Leah laughed. "Well, maybe she's had a change of heart."

"But why would she? It can't be because of you. You spent more time talking to Sarah and Julie than you did me," Megan said. "In fact, if I didn't know better, I would have thought you and Sarah were the ones who were dating."

"But, in all fairness to me, they—"

"Oh, my God! That's it! She knows you're not a threat." Megan turned to her, pointing a finger at her chest. "It's your fault! She knows we're not dating! That's why she was so damn nice! Because she *knows*."

Leah tried—unsuccessfully—to keep a smile from her face, causing Megan to poke her in the chest with her finger.

"I can't believe you find this funny!"

Leah laughed. "Maybe it's my age. It doesn't take much to amuse me."

Megan groaned. "I'm going to be so screwed. She's going to tell everyone. She's probably putting the nude photo out there right now. I'll be laughed out of town."

"Well, from what I've seen so far, you might be whistled out of town, but I don't think anyone would be laughing."

Megan narrowed her eyes. "I'm beginning to like you less and less."

Leah smiled but said nothing; she just continued on their walk toward the grill. The problem was, she was beginning to like Megan more and more. She sorely regretted not getting the opportunity for a kiss. Not necessarily the wet, sloppy fake kind that they'd teased about.

She admitted, though, that Megan probably had a point. Sarah and Julie had monopolized her time, leaving little for Megan. She hadn't wanted to be rude to them by ignoring their questions. Instead, she'd ended up being rude to her date by ignoring her.

"You're right," she conceded.

"Right? About?"

"It's my fault. I'm afraid I'm out of practice at dating," she said. "I guess I don't have the right mindset. We're pretending to date, yet we're not really dating. So...I wasn't quite as attentive as I should have been tonight." She paused on the sidewalk between her shop and the grill. "Two people newly dating would have been holding hands, touching, sitting together, and making goo-goo eyes at each other."

Megan laughed. "Goo-goo eyes, huh?"

"Yes. So I can see where the others might be confused."

Megan sighed. "Well, it's too late now."

Leah took a step closer. "Then I'll have to make good on my dinner invitation. We'll have to be much better actors the next time." She took Megan's hand and moved even closer. "So...I think we should practice."

Megan's eyes widened, but she didn't move away. Leah tugged Megan's hand as she leaned closer, gently brushing her lips against Megan's. She hesitated only a fraction of a second before kissing her again, this time letting her lips linger, surprised when Megan's lips parted, albeit slightly, as they moved against hers. She was also surprised by the quickening of her pulse, something she hadn't felt in many, many years.

Megan was the first to pull away, and Leah was sorry that she'd ended the kiss, although she reminded herself that they were on a public sidewalk. Probably not the best place to be "practicing" kissing.

"I...I should go," Megan murmured as she took a step away from her.

Leah caught her eyes, but only for a second as Megan turned and hurried toward the grill. Leah's gaze followed her, a slow smile forming on her face as Megan disappeared from sight. Damn, but that felt kinda good. Who would have thought she'd enjoy kissing Megan Phenix that much?

She sighed contentedly as she unlocked the door to her shop. She paused to look around, the light from the back casting enough glow for her to see the stuff she'd put out. She still wasn't used to the shop being nearly full and she supposed she needed to stop referring to her merchandise as "stuff." And even though she still had several things that hadn't come in yet, she had enough to go ahead and open the shop for business.

That thought made her pulse race nervously. A very different kind of racing than when she was kissing Megan. She much preferred the former.

CHAPTER TWENTY-SIX

Megan wasn't sure what was worrying her more…the fact that Leah had kissed her—and she'd actually kissed her back—or that Nancy wasn't home yet. She punched her pillow once again, then glanced at the clock. The midnight hour had come and gone. Where the hell was Nancy? More importantly… what the hell was Mary Beth doing to her?

Was she stripping her naked, taking pictures? Was she posing her in her bed, planning for her next Facebook attack? She smiled a little, thinking it would serve Nancy right, considering how unconcerned she was about *her* pictures being out there.

"And what was up with that kiss?"

Was it practice, like Leah had suggested? Had someone perhaps seen them and reported it back to Mary Beth? She stared up at the dark ceiling, reliving the kiss once again. She closed her eyes as she felt a rush, then opened them again.

"That's crazy," she murmured. "I don't even *like* her."

She rolled over onto her side, tucking one hand beneath her chin. How had her life become so complicated? How had her simple, boring, single life turned into all this? Well, she blamed Mary Beth, of course. But part of the blame should fall to Erin too. It was her phone call that drove her to…tequila. Yes, it was the tequila's fault too. And Nancy and her damn surprise birthday party. Yeah…it was really all Nancy's fault, if she thought about it. Had she not had a birthday party for her, none of this would have happened.

"Yeah…let's blame Nancy," she whispered into the darkness. She leaned up and looked at the digital clock on her nightstand. It was twelve forty-two. How long should she wait before she called Mary Beth? *Should* she call Mary Beth? When the roles were reversed, Nancy hadn't bothered to call and check on her whereabouts. That thought sealed it, and she burrowed into the pillow again, vowing to quit worrying about Nancy.

"So…what was up with that kiss?"

* * *

Megan was shocked to find Nancy in the kitchen the next morning, standing by as the Keurig did its magic. Was she actually humming as she waited for the coffee?

Megan stood next to her, eyebrows raised expectantly. Nancy's sleepy eyes blinked several times.

"What?"

Megan put her hands on her hips. "And when did you finally come home? I was worried sick!"

"Gee, Mom, I wasn't aware that I had a curfew," Nancy said.

"If you weren't at a crazy woman's house—a crazy woman with a camera—I wouldn't have worried," she said. "Do we need to check Facebook?"

Nancy laughed. "You should be the one worried about Facebook. Mary Beth is convinced that you and Leah are nothing more than friends. In fact, she doubts that you're even friends."

Megan feigned indignation...or at least she hoped she did. "What in the world are you talking about?" she asked.

"She thinks you're faking it," Nancy said bluntly. "They all do."

"Faking? *Really?* Fake date?" She laughed, hearing her own nervousness. She widened her eyes, pretending to be shocked. "That's ridiculous. Even *I* wouldn't do something that crazy. Why would they even think that?"

"Well, come on, you two hardly spoke to each other at dinner," Nancy said.

"That's because Sarah and Julie were all over her! My God, they were fawning over her!"

Nancy took a sip of her coffee, then stepped aside, giving Megan room. Megan hastily put her own cup under the receptacle and grabbed a pod from the rack, noticing that her hand was shaking.

"There's also the fact that you don't date," Nancy said. "Ever. Julie and Sarah can both attest to that. So for you to accept Leah's invitation without your usual course of action has raised some questions."

"That's crazy," she muttered.

"You have to admit, it's a little weird that you're dating," Nancy said. "You made it no secret that you didn't like Leah. In fact, you couldn't even stand to be around her."

"I think that's a little strong," she said. "She was annoying, yes. But it was only because of the parking thing. The more I'm around her...well, she's kinda grown on me. As you went on and on about in the beginning...she's really nice."

"She's also older than you."

"So?"

"So...Tammi was three years younger than you were. Erin was ten years younger. Leah is eleven years older than you."

"Right. And maybe I've learned my lesson with younger women. It's actually refreshing being with someone mature. Compared to Erin, Leah is light years ahead in maturity."

Nancy eyed her suspiciously. "Has she kissed you yet?"

Megan couldn't believe she felt a blush light her face as if she were a schoolgirl getting questioned by her mother.

"I don't know that it's any of your business," she said curtly. "And it's certainly not Mary Beth's business."

Nancy laughed. "I haven't seen you blush in years. Is that a yes?"

CHAPTER TWENTY-SEVEN

Leah was nearly giddy as she made her first sale...a wind chime and a T-shirt. The T-shirt was off the "sale" rack that Megan had suggested.

"Thank you," she said as she slipped a business card for Ruby's into the sack. "Come back any time."

"You have quite a collection of things here. I've enjoyed browsing," the woman said.

"Thanks. More is on the way."

There was only one other person in the shop, and Leah went to the door, trying to give the woman some space. She'd left the front door open, and she stood there, watching her now "open" flags blowing in the breeze. Actually, whipping around might be more appropriate. She went out onto the sidewalk and looked to the sky, seeing dark clouds building. The predicted thunderstorms would no doubt hit them within the hour. Seeing dark clouds hovering overhead on her first day open was a little scary—she hoped it wasn't an omen.

She turned her gaze toward the Phenix Grill, seeing the lunch crowd beginning to arrive. She hadn't seen or spoken to Megan since Tuesday night when they'd parted company right here on the sidewalk. Parted with a kiss, she reminded herself. Although she really didn't need reminding. It was something that crossed her mind quite often. It was one of the reasons she hadn't gone over to see Megan. It was also the reason she decided to go ahead and open up shop. She needed something to keep her mind—and body—occupied. She was a little disappointed, though, that Megan hadn't come over. Surely she'd already seen her signs stating that she was open.

"Ma'am?"

She turned and went back inside, smiling at the younger woman who stood at the register with a pile of T-shirts. "Sorry. Just checking on the weather. Looks like rain is coming."

"I hope the weekend is nice," the woman said. "I just got into town yesterday evening. The rest of my party is coming tonight. We plan on doing some kayaking over the weekend."

"Really? Where do you go?"

"We're doing the White River first. Then we'll do the King's River. It's sort of an annual thing for us," she said. "Do you kayak?"

Leah shook her head. "It looks fun, it's just not something I've tried before."

"Oh, you should try it. It's addicting." The woman motioned to the shirts on the counter. "I've been in almost every shop in town and it's nice to see that you have some different T-shirts. Nearly everyone else sells the same thing."

"Well, thanks," Leah said. "Although a lot of the vendors sell the same thing too."

"Oh, my God! You're actually *open*?"

The woman's eyes widened at the outburst as she turned to the door, but Leah laughed. "That's the neighbor from over at the Phenix Grill," she explained as Megan stood in the doorway.

"Oh. I love that place," the woman said. "Great burgers."

Megan held her hand up apologetically. "Sorry. I didn't know you had a customer."

Leah rang up the T-shirts and took the woman's credit card, glancing up from time to time as Megan walked around the shop.

"Enjoy your kayaking trip," Leah said as she placed the receipt and a business card inside the bag. "I hope the weather's nice."

"Thanks. I'll probably bring my friends in here. They're always in the market for new T-shirts."

Leah nodded. "Thank you. I'd appreciate that."

As soon as the customer left, she pointed to the sales rack of T-shirts. "Excellent idea, by the way."

"Good." Megan raised both hands questioningly. "So when did you open?"

Leah shrugged. "I got brave enough to put my flags out this morning." She smiled and held up two fingers. "Two people came in, and they both bought something."

"You're on a roll then," Megan said with a smile. "Are you going to hire someone to work here?"

"To help me handle all my customers?" She laughed as she looked around the empty store. "I think I can manage."

But Megan shook her head. "You can't be here all the time. Not seven days a week," she said.

"I live here. Where else would I be?"

"What about when you need to go grocery shopping? Run errands? You can't be here all the time, Leah."

"I guess I hadn't really thought that far ahead," she said. She'd been so concerned with her inventory—and with whether she'd have any customers—that hiring a part-time worker hadn't crossed her mind.

"Well, not to get into your business, but Eileen's Aunt Dee is looking for work," Megan said. "Her husband recently retired, and I think he's driving her crazy being at home all the time."

"Oh…okay," she said hesitantly.

Megan laughed. "She's seventy-two and very, very sweet. And she makes the best oatmeal raisin cookies you'll ever eat."

"Well, I guess that alone is reason to hire her," Leah said. "Tell Eileen to ask her to come over. I'll visit with her and see what I think."

"Okay, I will."

Leah shoved her hands in the pockets of her shorts. "So… are you mad at me?"

Megan raised her eyebrows. "Mad?"

Leah shrugged. "You know…"

"Oh. Because you kissed me?" Megan shook her head. "No. I suppose it was necessary. I mean…someone was probably watching. That's good."

Leah nodded. "Yeah…but I don't know if anyone saw us. Sarah came by yesterday."

"Oh?"

"She asked me out. For dinner."

Megan's eyes widened. "Are you kidding me? The nerve!"

Leah smiled. "Guess where she asked me to go?"

Megan put her hands on her hips. "To Craig's?"

"If only."

Megan laughed. "El Gallo?"

Leah nodded. "Yep. Tex-Mex."

Megan's smile faltered. "Did you accept?"

"Of course not. What kind of a girlfriend would that make me?"

"Well, according to Nancy, they all think we're lying about that anyway," Megan said.

"Oh, yeah?"

"Apparently we didn't have enough interaction at dinner." Megan walked over to the chimes, touching them absently, bringing them alive. "I haven't heard from Mary Beth, though. Maybe you were right. Maybe she has grown tired of her game."

"Well, then maybe you'll get to break up with me sooner than you thought," she teased, although she hoped that wasn't the case. She would certainly miss her interactions with Megan.

"Or maybe it's the calm before the storm. She's up to something. I can feel it. She's been *too* quiet."

"Well, I for one am not ready to break up with you," she said honestly. "This arrangement was supposed to benefit both of us, remember. I don't relish having to dodge dates from Sarah or Julie. I'd just as soon they think you and I are madly in love and leave me alone."

Megan met her gaze. "If that's what you're hoping for, then we've been doing a horrible job of convincing anyone, I'm afraid."

"Well, we'll have to try harder then. Let's do dinner. Here, at my place," she said, repeating her earlier suggestion. "We'll do it Tuesday night, like Mary Beth did. That is, if you and Nancy can both get away from the grill again."

Megan nodded. "Shouldn't be a problem. It's right next door, if they need us."

"Great."

"Will you need help with dinner? I could have Johnny—"

"No, no…I'll whip up something," she said, already mentally going over her choices.

"Okay." Megan paused. "Will I see you this weekend?" She looked away quickly. "I mean, you know, for appearances' sake and all."

"Sure. I'll pop over for dinner." Leah tilted her head, watching Megan for a few seconds. "You know, you could always come over here after you close. Wind down with a glass of wine or something," she suggested.

Their eyes held, and in that brief—but intense—stare, she acknowledged the change that seemed to be taking place between them. She wondered if Megan recognized the transformation herself.

Megan finally nodded. "That sounds good. Tomorrow."

"Sure. But I'll probably come by for a burger tonight," she said. "In all my excitement of opening the store, I'm not sure I'm going to have any desire to cook dinner."

Megan smiled. "Well, I'm glad you're finally open. At least the parking spaces aren't going to waste any longer."

Leah nodded and smiled too. "Yeah. Send some of your customers this way, will you?"

Megan turned to go, then stopped. "You should hang some chimes outside. Maybe a windsock or two."

"Okay. A couple of windsocks would probably do the trick." She grinned. "You know, if I'm trying to piss Sarah off."

Megan laughed. "Sarah's store is so stuffed with socks and flags, it's hard to even shop there."

"She must do okay since that's all she sells," Leah said.

"I suppose. Well, see you later."

Leah watched her leave, her gaze following her progress as she walked the sidewalk toward the grill. She was a bit puzzled by Megan's visit. Was it really for appearances' sake that Megan wanted to see her this weekend? Surely it was. Even though she found herself enjoying Megan's company, that didn't mean it was reciprocated. Megan's sole goal was to get Mary Beth off her back. And Leah reminded herself that her goal was to deter any potential suitors. She had no desire to fall into the dating trap again. At her age, she was perfectly happy being single. And she was perfectly happy pretending to date someone in order to remain single.

"Yes, I am."

So with that, she turned her gaze from the now empty sidewalk and tried to think of what she could serve for dinner next week. A loud rumble of thunder brought her attention back outside, however. She watched as the first raindrops fell, then went over to the door and closed it as the thunderstorm approached.

CHAPTER TWENTY-EIGHT

The beer Megan was pouring spilled over the glass as she stared. Leah was in shorts and really, should a fifty-one-year-old have legs that nice? Maybe there was something good to say about biking after all. She pulled her eyes away and mentally shook her head. No, she wasn't *attracted* to Leah Rollins. She could admire someone's body without being attracted to them. She did acknowledge, however, that she seemed to forget when she looked at her that she didn't really like the woman.

"Here you go," she said, placing the beer in front Daniel, one of her regulars. "Where's your wife? She coming later?"

"No. Her sister's visiting. They went over to Branson today."

"Lucky you," Megan said with a laugh. "You were spared that misery, huh?"

"I can think of a hundred things I'd rather do on a Saturday than go on up to Branson," he said. "Like fishing."

"Was the river up after that thunderstorm yesterday?" she asked. "I heard they got over three inches up near Beaver."

"It was flowing pretty good," he said. "Caught a couple of nice trout though."

She felt Leah's presence and turned, smiling at her. "Hey."

"Hi. The place is packed already. Mind if I sit at the bar?"

Megan motioned down to an empty barstool, then patted Daniel on the arm. "Let me know when you want a refill."

"Thanks, Megan."

She moved down in front of Leah. "Beer?"

"Sure."

Megan took a frosted mug from the freezer. "I guess the thunderstorm yesterday kept you away," she said. "Did you manage dinner on your own?"

Leah nodded. "I keep a stash of frozen burritos on hand. Wasn't quite as good as a burger would have been."

"Well, not that I'm drumming up business for other places, but the pizza joint on Cliff Street delivers," she said as she placed the mug in front of Leah.

"Thanks, I'll keep that in mind." She took a sip, meeting Megan's eyes over the rim of the glass. "You still coming over tonight?"

Megan nodded. "I was planning on it. Unless you have other plans."

Leah smiled. "I've fended off another dinner invitation."

"Julie?"

"No. Carla."

"From the art gallery? I thought she'd asked you out before."

Leah shook her head. "Tony was trying to set me up with her. I guess she got tired of waiting on me to make the first move." Leah shrugged. "Anyway, I told her you and I were dating, which she'd already heard." She drank from her beer again, then laughed. "She said she'd been asking you out for years and you always turned her down. She wanted to know my secret."

Megan leaned on the bar, smiling. "And what did you tell her?"

"Well, I told her it was my witty charm that you couldn't resist."

"Oh, you're so right," Megan laughed. "It has *nothing* whatsoever to do with me stealing my parking spot back."

Leah pretended to be offended. "What? That's the reason you're going out with me? Hoping I'll cave and give you your spot back?"

"Of course. Why else would I tolerate you?" She looked past her. "Nancy's coming over," she murmured.

"Why, Leah, I didn't see you sneak in," Nancy said as she pulled out the barstool next to her and sat down.

"Hi, Nancy," Leah said. "I haven't seen much of Megan this week so I thought I'd pop over and visit. And get a burger," she added.

"You don't have to be here every night, you know," Nancy said, looking at Megan. "If I start dating someone, I plan to take a couple of nights off myself."

Megan stared at her and frowned. "You *never* date. Who are you going to start dating?" She was surprised by the blush on Nancy's face, and she raised her eyebrow.

"I'm simply saying that if I do start to date, that's all. So you should take some nights off. Having Leah come over here is not exactly what I'd call a date," Nancy said.

"I agree," Leah said. "Although she is coming over to my place after you close up tonight."

"Then why wait?" Nancy asked. "We can handle closing perfectly fine without you."

"My turn to tend bar," Megan reminded her.

Nancy laughed. "You tend bar every night. If Clint needs help, I'll do it."

"You hate tending bar."

"And you hate food prep, but you do it sometimes," Nancy countered. "Go on. Take the night off."

Megan glanced at Leah. It was one thing to go over to her apartment after closing and stay for an hour. Quite another to go over and stay four or five hours. Whatever in the world would they do for that long?

"Sounds great," Leah said. Then she smiled. "Can I still get a burger?"

"Sure. I'll grab something for me too. Be right back," Megan said.

* * *

"Thanks for making her do this," Leah said.

"I know she feels obligated to be here since I'm here," Nancy said. "Even when she and Erin were dating, she rarely took a night off." She leaned closer. "I'm sure that's what drove Erin to cheat on her. Megan wasn't available much."

"Well, I'll try to be more understanding of her work schedule," she said. "And speaking of that, I'm going to have a dinner party on Tuesday. Can you make it?"

Nancy nodded. "Yes. Mary Beth mentioned it to me. I'm sure you're excited to finally be opened. I'm looking forward to seeing your shop."

"Yes, it was exciting when the first customer came in yesterday. I had a total of two before the rain hit," she said with a laugh. "Thankfully, today was much better."

"Once June comes around and the town is crawling with tourists, you'll be plenty busy," Nancy said. "If I could offer a suggestion though…on nights when we have a live band, you might want to stay open later than usual. There's a lot of foot traffic on those nights and most of the other shops have already closed up."

"Good idea. Thanks."

"Oh, and I heard that you were going to visit with Eileen's aunt about a part-time job. Aunt Dee's a really sweet lady."

"I understand she makes good oatmeal raisin cookies too."

Nancy laughed. "Of course Megan would mention that. She loves her cookies."

"Well, until Megan mentioned it, I hadn't given any thought to hiring someone," she said. "It never occurred to me that I'd need help."

"You can't be there all the time," Nancy said, echoing Megan's words.

"Yeah, I realize that now. She said she would stop by tomorrow after church. She sounded nice on the phone."

"She is. And she used to work for Gwen Barksdale, so she has experience."

"Let's see…Gwen owns the Christmas store, right?"

"Right." Nancy leaned closer again, keeping her voice low. "Did you know she asked Megan out?"

"Who in town hasn't?"

Nancy laughed. "I know…but Gwen? She's sixty-five. Our mother is only sixty-four."

Megan walked up behind them. "Why are you telling her Mom's age?"

"Comparing her to Gwen Barksdale," Nancy said.

"*Really?* Must you?"

"Has she asked you out lately?" Nancy teased.

"No. But I did mention to her that *you* were much closer to her age. I think I also mentioned that to Mary Beth. Maybe you should be on the lookout, not me."

"Very funny." Nancy stood. "Well, I should let you two get going. Enjoy your dinner."

Leah eyed the bag she held. "That was quick."

"Well, I cut in line with my order," Megan said. "I can do that, you know."

"I would hope so. What'd we get?"

"I got you something different," Megan said. "Mediterranean burger."

"Sounds interesting."

"Veggie burger."

Leah nodded. "Okay, I'm game. What's on it?"

"The burger is made with chickpeas—garbanzo beans—and has roasted red pepper hummus, cucumbers, tomatoes, red onions and feta cheese," she said. "And a cucumber mayo that Johnny makes. You'll love his hummus too. He puts a little cayenne in. Gives it a nice bite."

Leah held the door open as they walked out onto the street. "I hope it's as good as you make it sound."

"It is. It's what I have most often," Megan said. "I rarely eat a real burger anymore."

"Seen too many of them?"

"Yes. I usually make a club sandwich for lunch with turkey and lots of veggies. I don't normally take time for dinner."

Leah unlocked her shop and motioned Megan inside.

"Unless Johnny has something left over from his lunch special," Megan continued.

"I would imagine I'd get sick of burgers too," she said as she locked the door again and led the way to the back stairs. She flipped on the light and paused before heading up. "Is this okay?"

"What do you mean?"

"Well, Nancy sort of forced dinner on us. I mean—"

"It's fine, Leah. Actually, taking a break from the grill is something both Nancy and I need. Saturday night is probably not the best night to be away, but it's nice to get a break."

"Good. Then I'll try to keep you entertained for a few hours."

"I wouldn't mind a good movie," Megan said. "That's something I never seem to have time for."

After getting them each a water bottle from the fridge, Leah sat next to Megan at the bar, forgoing the small dinner table. Leah pointed to it now.

"I've yet to use the table, but I guess it'll come in handy on Tuesday. I'll have to scrounge up two chairs though. I only have the four."

"You can use some from the grill," Megan offered as she pulled the burgers from the bag. She also produced a large container of onion rings.

"Oh, goody," Leah said as she grabbed one. "These are the best."

"As much as I'm sick of looking at burgers, I don't seem to get tired of onion rings."

Leah opened up her burger, seeing cucumbers and tomatoes bulging out on all sides. Fresh spinach leaves were shoved in too and she took a bite, surprised at how flavorful it was.

"This is great," she mumbled around a mouthful.

"Thank you," Megan said. "I hoped you'd like it."

Leah nodded. "I think I like it better than the pesto burger." She took a sip of her water. "Speaking of food, I've finally settled on what I'll have for dinner on Tuesday."

"Oh, yeah?"

"Fish tacos," she said. "I'll make up a beer batter and fry them. And I make a really good Baja sour cream sauce. Providing I can find fresh cilantro."

"You won't find it at Susie's. In fact, you'll only find frozen fish there too."

"Yeah, I know. So…I was thinking—"

"No," Megan said. "You cannot shop there."

"I don't understand these rules. If Susie doesn't offer what you need, what's the harm of shopping at the supermarket here? Why drive to Berryville?"

"Because locals support locals."

"But if she doesn't carry it, you have to shop elsewhere. It's like going to the Ford place and wanting to buy a Prius. They don't carry them. So…you have to shop someplace else."

"Believe me, I understand your argument. I had the same attitude when we first moved here. But locals support locals. If Susie doesn't carry something, you drive to Berryville. You don't shop at her competition here in town," Megan said. "The same with eating. Locals don't go to McDonalds for burgers. They come to the grill or, God forbid, the Burger Barn. They eat locally, they don't go to chain restaurants."

Leah sighed. "Okay, I get it. So where is Berryville, anyway?"

"Fifteen miles east. Takes about twenty minutes."

She reached for an onion ring. "So I guess you were right about me hiring someone. I can't be here all the time."

"Aunt Dee will be perfect for you," Megan said.

Leah nodded. "She's coming by tomorrow after church. Nancy said that she used to work for Gwen at the Christmas Store."

"She did. I think she also used to work for George and Peter down at their candle shop."

"So there won't be a whole lot of training involved." She laughed. "Maybe she can train me. It's not like I know what I'm doing."

"So how was it?"

"Better today. Friday, after the rain hit, I didn't have a soul come in. Today was actually kinda busy. It was fun."

"So no regrets yet on opening Ruby's?"

"Nope. Give me a year and we'll talk."

"What about moving here? Do you miss the city?"

Leah smiled. "I miss grocery shopping where I want to."

Megan laughed. "Besides that."

Leah shook her head. "Not really. It's taken me a while to get used to the slower pace. And get used to everyone knowing my business," she said with a laugh.

"What about friends?"

Leah shrugged. "I think when you move, you learn quickly if you were really close friends with someone or not. I had a group that I hung out with. I thought we'd keep in touch more, I guess." She took another onion ring and nibbled it. "A few phone calls, a couple of emails…that's about it. They're still hanging out, doing their thing. I'm an outsider now."

"I know what you mean. When we moved here, I had two really good friends that I thought I would *always* be friends with. Now? I can't even remember the last time we spoke," Megan said. "Interests change, priorities change and yeah, they're still there and you are suddenly out of the daily loop." She smiled. "So you make new friends."

Leah nodded. "Yeah. I make friends pretty easily. Having them over for dinner helps my cause too," she said with a grin.

"So the same group? Sarah and Julie too?"

"Yes. And I wondered if I should invite Carla. What do you think?"

Megan nodded. "Yes. Carla gets along fine with the others. In fact, I think Carla and Julie hang out some."

"Good. Then I'll have to borrow three chairs."

Megan leaned her elbows on the bar, studying her. Long enough for Leah to feel as if she were under a microscope. She finally raised her eyebrows questioningly.

Megan met her eyes and smiled. "You're nice," she stated. "That's why you make friends easily."

Leah shrugged. "Well, thank you. I think...you're nice too."

Megan laughed. "There's no need to lie."

Leah laughed too. "Well, when we first met, I may not have used that adjective to describe you. But now...at least to me, you're nice."

Megan studied her again. "You're too perfect."

"Perfect? I'm far from perfect," she said.

"No? Other than your obsession with parking spaces—which annoyed the hell out of me—I can't really find anything else wrong with you," Megan said. "You walk instead of drive. Or you ride your bike. You own an electric car. You're obviously conscientious about the environment. You're nice and polite to everyone. You're nearly perfect," she said again. Then she leaned closer and wiggled her eyebrows. "So what's wrong with you?"

Leah grinned. "I see...so you want to know what my faults are, is that it?"

"Yeah. Give me some."

Leah always hated this question. It ranked up there with strengths and weaknesses. If you listed off what you perceived to be weakness...then you sounded weak. And if you listed off your strengths, then you sounded arrogant.

"Well?"

"Okay. I like to take really long showers."

Megan wrinkled up her brow in a frown. "What? That's it? That's not a fault, Leah. Who doesn't like long showers?"

"I'm from California," she reminded her. "We kinda have a water shortage, you know. You don't take long, lingering showers there. But since I've been here, I've gone crazy with it."

Megan rolled her eyes. "Really? You can't come up with something better than that?"

Leah shrugged. "What about you? I mean, other than being obsessed with parking spaces," she teased.

"My faults? Oh, God…they're too numerous to name. I'm grouchy, for one. I'm opinionated. I'm always right. Everybody knows that." She paused. "But are those faults? That's just the way I am. That's just me." She smiled at Leah, a smile that she found infinitely sexy. "Do I have any faults? Maybe I don't."

Leah laughed. "Well, they say denial is the first step to acceptance."

"So you're saying I'm not perfect too? I told you that *you* were perfect."

Leah leaned closer, holding her eyes. "I suppose the longer we date, the more we'll find each other's faults. Then we can decide if we can live with them or not." She lowered her gaze to Megan's lips, watching in fascination as Megan's tongue poked out enough to wet them.

"Are we…are we still playing?" Megan asked softly, her voice hinting at nervousness.

Leah raised her gaze again, surprised to find Megan's eyes a bit darker than usual. Were they still playing? Teasing? Pretending?

"Because if we're still playing…don't you dare kiss me."

Leah smiled slightly. "So if I kiss you now, that means what? That it's not a fake kiss? That it's for real?"

"I'm finding it harder and harder to dislike you."

"That's because I'm perfect. You said so yourself."

When Megan's mouth lifted in a smile, Leah found she could no longer deny herself the kiss she wanted. A real kiss. She met Megan's eyes again.

"I'm not playing now," she murmured as she leaned even closer. She wouldn't have been surprised if Megan had backed away, rebuffing the kiss, but she didn't. And even though they'd kissed before, she still wasn't quite prepared for her heart to spring to life like it did. Maybe it was because Megan was being receptive to her kiss. Or maybe it was because Megan's mouth was impossibly soft. Or maybe it was the tiny moan that escaped Megan's lips when Leah deepened the kiss. Whatever the reason, she didn't want it to stop. But when she reached up to cup Megan's face to bring her closer, Megan pulled away.

"We...we can't do this," Megan said as she pushed her barstool back and stood up. "We...we just can't do this."

Leah was about to ask why, but Megan's frightened eyes caused her to pause. Why in the world would Megan be afraid? So, she said the first thing that popped into her mind.

"I'm sorry. I shouldn't have—"

Megan held her hand up. "Don't. I'm...it's me, Leah. Not you. And...I can't do this."

"Okay."

Megan was pacing now and Leah watched her with both amusement and curiosity.

"I don't do this," Megan said, motioning between them. "That's the reason for this...this arrangement between us." She pointed at Leah. "And *you* don't do this." Their eyes met. "I should go," Megan said hurriedly.

Leah stood up. "Look, I'm sorry I kissed you." She shoved her hands into her pockets, trying to appear less threatening as Megan took a step away from her. "But if we want this arrangement to work, then you probably should stay a while longer. You've been here less than an hour. I think that would raise a lot of questions."

Megan ran her hands through her hair. "You're right."

"So how about we find a movie to watch? You can take the sofa," she said. "And I'll take the recliner." Then she smiled, trying to lighten the moment. "That way, I'll be far enough away from you that I won't be tempted to kiss you."

Megan's shoulders sagged. "I'm sorry, Leah."

"Nothing to be sorry about," she said. "Find something to watch. I'll clean up our dinner."

"I'll help."

"Nope. I got it."

Really, there wasn't much to clean up, but Leah needed a few minutes to herself. She thought perhaps she'd misread Megan…but no, she recognized the look in her eyes for what it was. Regardless of the basis of the "arrangement" that they had between them, she wasn't blind to the fact that she was attracted to Megan. Surprised? Of course. It had been a very long time since she'd dated anyone. She hadn't been celibate all those years, but there'd never been anyone who made her heart quake from a simple kiss.

But Megan was probably right. They shouldn't do this. She was nearly twelve years older than Megan. What could Megan possibly see in her?

Nothing. Which is probably why she'd balked at the kiss.

Leah sighed, feeling a bit disappointed as the reality of their situation settled around her. They were fake dating. They were fake kissing.

Nothing more.

As she wiped off the bar, she glanced into the living room. Megan had taken her shoes off and was leaning back on the sofa, her feet curled under her. As she watched, Megan lifted her gaze, meeting her eyes. Leah suddenly wished that they weren't fake dating.

She wished it was for real.

CHAPTER TWENTY-NINE

Megan stood looking at herself in the mirror. Her hair was still wet from her shower, making it look darker than it really was. She tightened the towel a little tighter around her. She looked the same as she looked every morning after her shower. Except she felt different. As she met her dark eyes, she saw the change there.

It was…it was just a kiss. It was lips and mouths and nothing more. But then why did her heart still flutter when she thought about it? Why did she get a funny feeling in her stomach?

She closed her eyes, reliving the kiss one more time, remembering Leah's lips as they teased hers, feeling that same flutter in her chest as she had last night.

"God," she whispered. This wasn't supposed to happen. This was *so* not supposed to happen.

She met her eyes again. "I'm not attracted to her," she murmured. "I'm *not*."

She sighed. Who was she kidding? And when the hell did it happen?

She undid her towel and tossed it on the countertop. It didn't matter, she told herself. They would simply continue their little charade for the next few weeks...long enough for the others to be convinced that both she and Leah were off the market. Then they could gradually back off until they didn't have to see each other again. By then, summer would be bustling and there would be no time for all these little games.

In fact, maybe it was true. Maybe Mary Beth had already given up. There hadn't been another Facebook post. Mary Beth had not made good on her threat. Maybe Mary Beth was over it. If so, then maybe she and Leah could stop all this...this *pretending*.

Well, she didn't anticipate seeing Leah again until her dinner party on Tuesday. It was hard enough sitting through a two-hour movie together. Even though Leah had sat in the recliner, Megan had still felt her presence. And even though neither of them had mentioned the kiss, it was still there, hanging between them. The movie was a comedy. They'd laughed. They'd chatted. They'd ended the evening on a good note. But the kiss was still hanging between them. When the movie ended and she was getting ready to go, there'd been an uncomfortable silence in the room. She'd actually paused at the door, hoping that Leah would stop her, hoping that she might...what? Hug her? Kiss her again? Their eyes had held for a few seconds, seconds that seemed to last minutes. Long enough for her to see the indecision in Leah's gaze, long enough for her to realize that she really, really hoped Leah would move closer, would reach for her, would pull her into her arms. But none of that happened. Leah bid her a good night and Megan made her exit.

So no, she wouldn't see her again until Tuesday. At dinner, she would gauge Mary Beth's demeanor. If she felt like Mary Beth was no longer pursuing her, she'd simply tell Leah that their fake dating had worked, that it had served its purpose but it was no longer necessary to continue.

Yeah. That's what she'd do.

As she reached for her toothbrush, she met her eyes in the mirror once again. Yes, the sensible thing to do would be to end this…this fake *affair* with Leah. End it before it turned into something else entirely.

Sure…that's what she should do.

She looked away from the mirror. The problem was…it wasn't what she wanted to do.

"Oh, Megan…don't be stupid," she murmured.

Just end it and be done with it.

CHAPTER THIRTY

"You should go early and help," Nancy said.

"Why? She didn't ask me to," Megan said. That was true. She'd not seen Leah or even spoken to her since Saturday night. Saturday night and the kiss. "I know nothing about making fish tacos or Baja sauce, whatever that is."

Nancy stared at her. "You've been acting really weird the last few days. What's going on?"

"Nothing."

"Did you two have a fight or something?"

Megan laughed nervously. "A fight? What would we possibly have to fight about?"

"Well, seeing as how you haven't been dating that long, I wouldn't think there'd be anything to fight about. But I do remember how it was when you first met. The only conversation between you was an argument."

Megan shook her head. "I told you, I'm over the parking thing."

"Then what? Having second thoughts about dating?"

"Why? Are you still interested in her?"

"No. I'm way past that," Nancy said. "She's not my type, anyway."

Seeing as how Nancy hadn't dated anyone since they lived in St. Louis, she was about to ask *who* her type was but thought better of it. Her track record wasn't much better than Nancy's.

"Well, maybe you're right," she said instead as she stood up. "It would be nice of me to go over early and see if she needs help."

"Yes, it would. But before you go, there's something else I want to talk to you about."

Megan sat back down. "Okay. What's up?"

"I've been thinking that we…well, that we need to take some time off. Away from here."

Megan nodded. It was something she'd thought about too. "What do you have planned?"

"I think we should each take a day—a whole day—where we don't come in at all. Not just a morning off or an afternoon. Or even missing dinner once in a while. A whole day."

"Even during the summer?"

"Yes. I think we need a break. By the time August rolls around, we're both exhausted and crabby." She smiled. "Well, you're crabby most of the time anyway, but you get what I'm saying."

Yeah, Megan got what she was saying, and yes, they were both running on fumes by the time summer ended. She agreed with Nancy that they needed a break, but why now? What prompted this change? She narrowed her eyes. Something was going on. If she thought about it, for the last couple of weeks, Nancy had been …well, different. But she'd been too stressed about her own situation to be concerned with Nancy. But there was definitely something going on.

"Well?" Nancy asked. "What do you think?"

Megan nodded. "Okay. If that's what you want. But we're not talking weekends, right?"

"No. I was thinking Monday, Tuesday or Wednesday. Maybe even Sunday. We can pick a day."

Megan shrugged. "Okay. Fine by me."

Nancy smiled. "Good. I'll take Mondays, if that's okay."

Yeah…she was up to something. Only Megan didn't have a clue as to what it could be. But she nodded. She wasn't going to argue about having a day off.

"Fine. I'll let you know what day I want."

"Great. Now, go already. I'm assuming you're going home to shower and change first."

"Yeah." She stood again. "Well, I'll see you next door. About seven?"

"Yes."

Nancy was still smiling, and Megan left the office with a frown on her face. Something was going on…and she *hated* not knowing what the hell it was.

* * *

She was nervous as she drove back down the hill after her quick shower. Nervous and she wasn't exactly sure why. Afraid to be alone with Leah? Maybe. So in an act of defiance, she pulled into one of Ruby's parking spots—her old reserved spot—and that made her feel a little better. She was surprised, however, to find Ruby's still open. It was nearly six. Most shops didn't stay open past five until June.

She walked in the open door, pleased to see a few customers milling about. It wasn't Leah behind the counter, however.

"Aunt Dee? Are you working already?"

The older woman laughed. "I'm not sure if it was the good word you girls put in for me or the batch of oatmeal cookies I brought, but Leah hired me on Sunday and I started yesterday."

"Good for you," Megan said. "And how's Glen?"

"Oh, bless his heart. The man couldn't find the fridge without my help." Aunt Dee lowered her voice. "I told him either he went back to work or I was."

Megan laughed. "He's been retired a couple of months now?"

"Three. I can't get a thing done around the house. He's always underfoot."

"Well, I'm sure he'll adjust."

"Oh, I know. He needs to find him a hobby is all." Aunt Dee moved around her as a customer brought some things to the counter. "You're here for the dinner party, I guess."

Megan nodded. "Yes. I came early. Thought Leah might need some help."

"Go on up, dear. She asked me to stay late so she wouldn't have to lock up down here until all the guests arrived."

"Oh, okay." Megan headed for the stairs. "Good to see you again," she said, but Dee had already turned her attention to the customer.

As she turned the corner to go up the stairs, she paused, looking at each step as her gaze traveled up to the door at the top. She took a deep breath, trying to settle her nerves. It had been three days. She should be over it by now. Besides, Leah was obviously over it. It wasn't like she'd tried to contact her or anything.

Right. So it was no big deal. They'd kissed. Over and done with.

"No big deal," she murmured as she took the first step up. But still…it was going to be awkward between them. Surely it was. Maybe they needed to talk about it. Clear the air. Because if things were awkward, then Mary Beth would pounce. Surely she would.

She shook her head. She was being ridiculous and she knew it. They should be able to pull off this dinner party without any problem. Besides, Sarah or Julie—or both—would most likely occupy all of Leah's time anyway. Or Carla, she added as she continued up the stairs. Everyone wanted a date with Leah, it seemed. Well, the good thing about that was that they weren't asking *her* out any longer.

She paused at the door, then with another deep breath, she knocked three times.

"Come in. It's unlocked," Leah called from inside.

Megan opened the door, finding Leah in her kitchen with her back to the door. A quick glance told her Leah wasn't yet ready for company. She was in shorts and a paint-stained T-shirt.

"Hey," Leah said. "Come here. This needs something and I can't figure out what."

Megan went into the kitchen, obediently opening her mouth as Leah shoved a spoon inside.

"Well?"

Megan nodded. "Spicy."

"And?"

"It's good."

"What does it need?"

Megan smiled. "What is it?"

"It's the Baja sauce."

"Since I've never tasted it before, I have no idea if it needs anything."

"More cilantro?"

"No."

"A little more lime? Adobo sauce, maybe?"

"What do *you* think it needs?"

"Well, I would go with more chipotles, but not everyone likes things as spicy as I do." Leah smiled and wiggled her eyebrows teasingly. "If you know what I mean."

Megan laughed lightly, surprised that such a simple gesture put her at ease and chased away the nervousness she'd been feeling. Things were fine between them. There was no need to clear the air or talk about…the kiss.

"I wouldn't mind it being a little spicier," she said. "Spicy is good."

"A woman after my own heart, I see," Leah said with a grin. "What are you doing here already?"

"I thought you might need some help." She shrugged. "Nancy suggested it would be the proper thing to do."

"Ah. Well, I chopped the cabbage and made up a slaw already," Leah said. "I've seasoned the fish and it's marinating. So I'm good."

"What about the beer batter?"

"I'll stir that up right before I fry." She closed the lid on her Baja sauce and put it in the fridge. "Something to drink?"

"Just a water for now."

Leah took two bottles from the fridge and handed one to Megan. "I guess you saw Dee."

Megan nodded. "She seems excited to be working."

"Or excited to get away from her husband, I can't decide which," Leah said with a laugh. "But you were right. She's super nice. And she knows exactly what to do."

"How much will she work?"

"About twenty hours for now. During the summer, she's open to working more, and she doesn't mind working on Saturdays, so that's a plus."

"There were a few customers down there," she said. "Have you been pleased?"

Leah nodded. "We haven't been packed, by any means, but at least people are coming in to take a look. I've also had a few people from other shops come in, just to look around."

"Competition," she said. "And being nosy."

Leah leaned a hip against the counter. "So...everything okay? With us?"

Megan met her gaze, then nodded. "Yes. You?"

"Yeah. I didn't know if...well, if you thought we needed to talk or something."

"Do you think we need to talk?"

Leah studied her for a moment, then nodded. "Maybe."

Megan was surprised by her answer. "Maybe?"

Leah shoved off the counter. "Now's probably not the best time. I need to shower." She pointed toward the living room and TV. "Make yourself at home."

Megan stared after her as she walked away. *She's got really nice legs*, she thought. Then she shook her head, chasing that thought away as quickly as she could. Leah wanted to talk. What did she want to talk *about*? The kiss? Their fake dating? Was she going to break up with her?

But I'm not ready to break up.

She sat down heavily on the sofa and picked up the remote, flipping it around in her hands. She finally turned the TV on, more for background noise than anything else. Her mind was racing and she needed something to distract her. Unfortunately, the TV wasn't helping.

Leah wanted to talk…apparently.

CHAPTER THIRTY-ONE

Megan heard the water turn off and knew Leah was finished with her shower. And, okay, yes, she did picture Leah naked, dripping wet...yes, she did. But only for a few seconds. That didn't mean anything, she told herself.

When she heard movement in the bedroom, she got up and went over to the windows that faced Spring Street. She looked out, watching as a few tourists still lingered. Most of the shops had closed already, and she wondered how many of the people milling about were making their way over to the grill for dinner. Or perhaps they would stop into Ruby's since Aunt Dee was keeping it open later than usual.

"Anything interesting?"

She turned, finding Leah watching her. She was dressed in black jeans and a dark gray shirt that matched her hair perfectly.

"You...you look nice," Megan said.

"Thank you."

Leah came closer, and Megan took a shaky breath, not realizing that she'd been holding it. She clutched her hands together behind her back, meeting Leah's gaze.

"You mentioned that we should maybe talk," she said. They might as well get it over with before the others arrived.

"Yeah. Well, I think I've changed my mind," Leah said. "Let's just see where it goes."

Megan met those smoky gray eyes...or were they blue? "See...see where *what* goes?" she asked hesitantly.

As Leah leaned closer, Megan knew she was going to kiss her. Of course she knew that. And she should have taken a step back. She should have turned her head, at least. But she did neither of those things. With her hands still clutched behind her back, she squeezed her own fingers tightly when Leah's mouth met hers. It was a gentle, rather sweet kiss, and Megan had no desire to pull away from it.

"Let's see where *this* goes," Leah murmured, her mouth still mere inches away.

Megan blinked several times, her eyes locked on those lips that were far too close to her own. She finally took a step back, shaking her head to clear it.

"*What?* No," she said. She held her hands up in front of Leah as if to push her away. "We can't do this."

"Why? You said that the other night...but *why* can't we do this?"

"Because," she said, as if that one word explained everything. But there was a smile playing on Leah's lips, a smile she was trying to hide, it seemed. "Because we don't do this. We don't date," she said, trying again to explain. "We...this would be a terrible idea."

"But we're already dating," Leah said.

"We're *fake* dating!"

"So what if it's not fake dating. What if it's real dating?"

"Oh, my God! Are you serious? Why would you want to date me?"

"I like you."

Megan shook her head. "Why do you like me?"

Leah gave up on trying to hide her smile. "Why do you like *me*?"

"What makes you think I like you?"

Leah leaned closer again, and again, Megan failed to heed the warning bells sounding. The kiss was a little harder, a little longer, and Megan found herself responding to it once again.

"That's why," Leah whispered when she pulled away.

"Oh, my God," she murmured. "You're driving me freakin' crazy."

"Driving you crazy's a good thing, right? I mean, it's not like Mary Beth crazy. Is it?"

Megan couldn't help but laugh. "No." But her smile faded as she shook her head. "This is a terrible idea, you know."

"Is it?"

Megan's mistake was meeting Leah's eyes. Smoky gray or smoky blue—it didn't matter which. They were dark with desire, and even though Megan tried, she couldn't look away from them.

"Oh...*crap*," she whispered as she moved closer, sliding her hands up Leah's shoulders and around her neck. The gentle, almost playful kisses of earlier were chased away, replaced by such a passionate kiss, Megan would swear she felt the earth shake. Leah, only slightly taller than she was, pulled her in tight, their hips meeting and then their thighs. She lost herself for a moment as Leah's tongue brushed her own, causing her to moan, an embarrassingly loud moan which made her feel like a sex-starved virgin in a cheesy romance novel. The embarrassment wasn't enough, however, to make her pull away from the kiss. Quite the opposite, she pressed her body even closer to Leah, her mouth opening fully, her tongue trying to slip past Leah's and into her mouth. Yes, she felt utterly sex-starved—and she supposed she was—and later, she might be thankful to whoever was knocking on Leah's door, stopping her before she began ripping her clothes off. But right now, right this moment, she wanted to curse—and ignore—the interruption. Because her body was on fire, and when Leah pulled away, ending their heated kiss, she felt nearly delirious. Her eyes wouldn't focus, her legs felt weak and she was hot and feverish.

"Megan?"

She blinked several times, finally seeing through the cloudy haze in her eyes, realizing she was still holding on to Leah. More of the obtrusive knocking sounded and Leah smiled.

"I should probably get that, don't you think."

Megan wet her suddenly dry lips, running a hand through her hair. "Oh, my God. I can't believe that just happened. I'm…I'm sorry. I…I—"

Leah leaned closer and kissed her, her mouth moving slowly across her lips, silencing her. "It did happen. We kissed," she said quietly. "It was a really good kiss, Megan. Don't apologize." Then she smiled. "And don't fight it. I hope we have many more like that."

Megan stood there, still in a state of shock as Leah walked across the room to the door. She turned her back to the door and stared out the windows instead, trying to regain some semblance of normalcy. They kissed. That's all. Just a kiss. People did that all the time. *Kissed.*

She took a deep breath, absently hearing Leah as she greeted Nancy and Mary Beth. Nancy would take one look at her and know immediately what the delay was in Leah opening the door. She'd know that they'd been kissing. Of course, that didn't really matter. She and Leah were supposedly dating. They kissed. She felt the now familiar flutter in her stomach as she recalled the fiery kiss, but she had no time to reflect on it. Laughter in the room caused her to turn from the window as Sarah and Julie had joined them.

Only then did it occur to her odd that Nancy and Mary Beth had arrived together. Well, they were friends. She supposed Mary Beth had popped over to the grill and they'd walked over.

Nancy elbowed her playfully. "You look all flushed, sis," she teased. "Did we interrupt something?"

Despite her attempt not to, Megan felt a red-hot blush cover her face, causing Nancy to laugh. It would do no good to protest so she nodded and smiled.

"Yes, you did, actually."

Nancy's expression turned serious. "Good for you. I like Leah. She's the complete opposite of Tammi and Erin."

She nodded. "Yes, she is."

"And I don't only mean her age. She's...different."

"Mature."

"Well, that too, but...I don't know. Different."

Megan smiled. "Glad you approve."

She would admit that the evening was a little less stressful than last week's dinner at Mary Beth's, but only slightly. Gone was the fear that the others would find out that they were fake dating. That was replaced with the fear that they were going to *really* date. A handful of times she found her gaze drifting to Leah, and more often than not, she would find Leah's eyes already on her.

God...what the hell were they doing?

Instead of expensive wine and margaritas, Leah served cold Corona beer with lime wedges and a jug of fruity sangria. Megan enjoyed the beer but thought she would try the sangria with the fish tacos.

As was the case at Mary Beth's, she found herself relegated to the background as Sarah and Julie again fought for Leah's attention. Megan found it a bit amusing as they peppered Leah with questions. Nancy and Mary Beth were sitting together on the sofa, and Megan noticed that Mary Beth no longer had that coy smile or predatory look in her eyes. That was a relief. Maybe she wouldn't be exposed on Facebook after all.

"I should get the fish going," Leah said as she walked over to the bar where Megan was sitting. "Feel like helping?"

"Yes."

She went around the bar and into the kitchen, ignoring the chatter from the living room. "I thought Carla was coming," she said.

"So did I. Maybe she changed her mind."

Leah already had a pan filled with oil on the stove, and she turned that on. "If you would open a beer for me, I'll add that to the batter."

Megan did as requested, then stood back as Leah went to work frying the fish. She was quick and efficient, and Megan smiled as she leaned against the counter. "You really didn't need my help, did you?"

Leah smiled too. "Back in the old days, I used to make fish tacos at least once a week." She looked over at her, holding her gaze for a few seconds. "But I did want your company."

The look in her eyes made Megan's pulse race, and in a flash, she recalled being pressed against Leah, their thighs touching, their hips in a far too intimate position, their kiss— long and passionate—perhaps a precursor of things to come.

She suddenly felt hot and she took a step away from Leah on shaky legs. To her surprise, Leah turned to her, her eyes a smoldering shade of blue and gray. For a second, Megan forgot about the others. She couldn't look away from Leah's gaze, and she barely fought the urge to kiss her. Leah, however, had no such luck resisting as she leaned closer, kissing her just hard enough to elicit a tiny moan from Megan.

"Need help in here? I smelled something burning, but I guess it's not the fish, is it?" Nancy teased and Megan pulled away from Leah with a guilty blush.

"Very funny," Megan said as she cleared her throat. "I was…I was helping, you know…with the—"

"Well, if we're ever going to eat, I think you should let me help," Nancy said as she pushed Megan out of the kitchen.

Leah laughed. "Thanks. She *is* distracting."

Megan had no choice but to go out and join the others. Julie and Sarah were in a two-way conversation, discussing the merits of a rumor going around that Melissa and Carla were seen sneaking around together.

"She would have told me," Julie insisted. "We're friends."

"I can't see it," Sarah said. "They don't go together at all."

Megan tuned them out and turned to Mary Beth who was sitting on the sofa. She patted the space beside her and Megan gave a silent groan as she went to sit.

"You look frightened."

"Yes. You tend to do that to me," Megan said bluntly.

Mary Beth laughed. "No, not me. I meant her," she said, motioning toward the kitchen.

"Leah? Why would I be frightened of Leah?"

"I think you're afraid you're going to fall in love with her."

Megan was shocked by her words. Was Mary Beth conceding defeat? She should graciously accept the statement and move on, but she felt the need to clarify. "We hardly know each other, really. I don't think falling in love is on the table."

Mary Beth surprised her by patting her knee in an almost motherly way. "Let me give you some advice, young Megan. Sometimes love comes from such unexpected places. You find it's been there all along, right in front of you."

Megan frowned. Were they still talking about her? Did that statement warrant a response? Before she could comment, Mary Beth continued.

"Yes, right in front of you. Sometimes it takes something extraordinary to bring it to the surface. And other times, love hits you out of the blue. A stranger comes and changes your life. Like you and Leah." She smiled at Megan. "Love comes in different ways, different packages...but I say, when it comes, you better grab it. Don't be afraid. None of us are getting any younger, you know."

Megan had absolutely no idea what Mary Beth was rambling on about, and she wondered if maybe she'd had too many Coronas. Before she could respond, there was a knock on the door. Megan rose to get it, but Julie beat her to it. It was Carla.

"Hey, everyone. Sorry I'm late."

Carla looked a bit flushed, and Sarah and Julie exchanged knowing glances. Megan looked at Mary Beth, but her gaze was focused on the kitchen—and Nancy. Everything seemed suddenly very weird.

* * *

Megan managed three fish tacos and she blamed the Baja sauce. She could eat that stuff with a spoon.

"I love the spicy cabbage slaw," Sarah said. "You've got to give me the recipe."

"Sure. It's easy," Leah said as she started gathering plates.

"Let me help," Megan offered.

There were only two pieces of fish left, and she found herself eyeing them. "Put those somewhere before I eat them," she said to Leah.

Leah laughed. "I take it you liked the tacos."

"Delicious," she said. "Everything was great."

Leah leaned closer. "I saw you and Mary Beth chatting. Is she threatening another Facebook post?"

Megan shook her head. "No. She didn't mention it. She's acting really weird. It's like she doesn't have any interest in me at all."

"That's a good thing, right?"

"Oh, yeah! That would be fantastic. It's just kinda weird how she stopped, you know."

"So maybe she stopped because of me."

"Maybe so. But she was rambling. She was going on and on about all the different ways to fall in love." She met Leah's eyes. "Call me crazy, but…" she motioned to the living room where Mary Beth and Nancy were again sitting on the sofa together. "You don't think she and Nancy are, you know…" But she shook her head. "*No*. Not Nancy. She wouldn't. No."

They were both watching as Mary Beth leaned closer to Nancy, whispering something, something that caused Nancy to laugh like a schoolgirl. Megan's eyes widened and she grabbed Leah's arm.

"Oh. My. *God*," she hissed. "They're making goo-goo eyes at each other!"

Leah laughed, then leaned over and kissed Megan quickly on the mouth. "I find you adorable, by the way."

Megan's head was spinning, and she leaned against the counter. Mary Beth and *Nancy*? Carla and *Melissa*? And now Leah found her *adorable*? What's next? Were Julie and Sarah on the verge of *dating*?

She looked over at Leah, who was humming as she wiped off the counter. Her gaze slid to the living room, bouncing from Mary Beth and Nancy to Julie and Sarah, who were still sitting at the table chatting. Carla was on her phone texting, seemingly oblivious to everyone around her.

"What in the hell is happening here?" she murmured.

CHAPTER THIRTY-TWO

Leah stood at the windows looking down on Spring Street long after Megan had left. Strange, but she could still feel the younger woman's presence, could still feel Megan's body as they'd hugged tightly. And she could still hear the trepidation in Megan's voice.

"This is a terrible idea, you know."

She smiled now, recalling their conversation. As soon as the others had left, leaving her and Megan alone, she'd sensed Megan's nervousness.

"You okay?"

Megan had nodded. "Yes. No." Then a smile. "I'm not sure."

Leah hadn't been able to resist. "Come here." She'd pulled Megan into her arms, squeezing her tightly, securely, trying to let her know that everything would be fine. She'd felt Megan's arms snake around her waist, tightening their hold too.

"You give nice hugs," Megan had murmured against her neck.

"Thanks. You're kinda nice to hug."

"Are we really going to do this?"

"I think so." She'd pulled back enough to meet Megan's gaze. "What is it you're afraid of?"

Megan had slipped out of her arms and moved a few steps away from her. When their eyes met again, Leah had glimpsed a bit of sadness mixed in with the fear she saw there.

"I don't have a great track record. In fact—"

"Megan…I'm not Tammi or Erin. I'm fifty-one. Too damn old for games." She'd shoved her hands into her pockets, her turn to fight nervousness. "I'm attracted to you. I think you're attracted to me. Let's just see where this goes."

The fear left Megan's eyes, but the sadness did not. "I've been hurt," she'd said, tapping her chest. "I don't want to go through that again."

She moved from the window finally, going back into her empty apartment. What was it she hoped to accomplish here? Should she heed Megan's warning…that it was a terrible idea that they date? Should they just forget about it? She supposed the fake dating had served its purpose. Mary Beth had apparently moved on in her quest to date Megan…moved on to her sister. Was there still a need for them to date?

The truth was, the more time she spent with Megan, the more time she wanted. She didn't want it to be fake dating. She wanted it to be real.

She shook her head and ran a hand through her hair. Real? This coming from the woman who hadn't dated anyone in *years*? Why would she want to complicate her life like that? She was content. She'd already resolved herself to being alone. Dating was a chore. Dating brought complications. And sometimes— as both she and Megan could attest—dating brought heartache. Did she want to take a chance again? To what end? Sex?

She shook her head once more. If it was only sex she wanted, she could get that without all the drama of dating someone. Isn't that how she'd existed for the last umpteen years? Did she really want to disrupt her life by adding someone to it? She was just getting started with Ruby's. She had her hands full there. June was right around the corner. June brought lots of tourists.

Was there even any time to date someone? And Megan…as busy as the grill was, could she find the time to spare for dating?

No. Megan was probably right—it was a terrible idea.

Yeah. Neither of them had time to devote to this. Not to real dating. Maybe they should stick to what they'd been doing. Fake dating. It would be a whole lot simpler.

But there was that kiss.

She nodded. "Yeah…there was that kiss."

CHAPTER THIRTY-THREE

"Since when are you attracted to older women?"

Her reflection in the mirror didn't answer her, and Megan sighed as she tossed the towel down. Yes, Leah was older. But if not for her head full of lovely gray hair, you'd never guess she was over fifty. Did that matter? Age should be irrelevant. It *was* irrelevant. It wasn't like she'd consciously discounted anyone who was older than she was as potential dates. There simply wasn't anyone in town she'd been even remotely interested in. But when Erin waltzed into town—ten years younger than she was—and started flirting with her, hadn't she been secretly pleased that there was finally someone closer to her own age asking her out?

Yes, she had been. Of course, at the time, she failed to see how immature Erin really was. Well, ignored it was closer to the truth. And as she'd told Leah, she knew it was going nowhere with Erin...she *knew* it. Yet...she kept dating her because Erin was cute and young and she made Megan feel cute and young.

"God, you're pathetic," she murmured to her reflection.

What in the world was she going to do? She'd never dated anyone older than she was. Never. Not even in college. Why was she having such a hard time with this? Fake dating was suiting them just fine. Why complicate things by making it real?

"Because that kiss was real," she whispered. Damn, that kiss practically made her knees buckle. When had that ever happened?

"Never."

She sighed again. That, of course, was the problem. That damn kiss had her running scared. She had nothing to compare it to. She'd been only twenty-four when she and Tammi moved in together. Tammi was barely twenty-one. Their relationship had been based almost entirely on sex, yet she couldn't recall a single time that a kiss from Tammi had affected her this way. And Erin? *Please*. It wasn't kisses she was after with Erin. After being celibate for over eight years, kissing was the last thing on her mind.

She shook her head slowly as she pulled out her toothbrush. Was that it? She was thirty-nine years old and she had two so-called relationships to her name and, sadly, both had been based on sex. Was that it?

And now here was Leah, an attractive, older woman who made her knees buckle and her heart flutter from a kiss. What would making love with her be like?

Her eyes widened as she met them in the mirror. Would Leah turn her world upside down? Would Leah's touch send her spinning out of control? Would the sex be wild and crazy? Or would it be slower, gentler?

Would Leah make her fall in love with her?

She dropped her toothbrush into the sink as her hands gripped the countertop tightly. Is that what she was afraid of? Had Mary Beth's ramblings about falling in love gotten to her?

"Jesus, you're not even *dating* yet," she reminded herself. Yet, as Leah had said, they *were* dating, weren't they? That kiss certainly said they were dating.

"This is a terrible idea."

That didn't seem to matter though. If she were honest with herself, she'd admit that she liked Leah. She liked being around her. Leah made her smile, made her laugh. There was absolutely no reason *not* to date her. And being afraid that her kisses would buckle her knees was not a valid reason.

Being afraid that she might fall in love with Leah...yeah, that was a valid reason. But she had absolutely no intention of falling in love with anyone.

But damn...that kiss felt good. That kiss made her feel alive.

"You're in such big trouble," she murmured.

CHAPTER THIRTY-FOUR

Leah stood at the door, watching the rain come down. Having lived her whole life in the Bay Area, she rarely saw good old-fashioned thunderstorms like this. Water was running down the street, splashing against the curb as people took cover in the shops along Spring Street. Unfortunately, none of them chose Ruby's for their shelter. She watched a little longer, then a streak of lightning overhead sent her back into her shop seconds before thunder shook the windowpanes.

The locals seemed to take these thunderstorm watches and warnings in stride. Even tornado watches didn't seem to faze them. She, however, had no such experience with this so when she woke that morning to an alert on her phone—possibility for severe weather, including tornadoes—she had gone into panic mode. She had no designated safe room, no survival kit packed, no exit strategy. Then she had to remind herself that it wasn't an earthquake she had to prepare for.

She would check with Megan and Nancy and see how they handled these situations. What did they do when the grill was full and a storm came in? What did they do at their house? Did they have a room they could take shelter in? She glanced around her shop, knowing the only safe place would be her storage room. It was in a back corner and it had no windows. That's where she would go.

As another boom of thunder sounded, she wondered if she should go there now. But what if a customer came in?

"In this mess?"

She could barely see across the street, and the wind was blowing the rain sideways. No one was going to come in until the storm passed. Still, she hesitated. Maybe she was overreacting. It was only a thunderstorm. A severe thunderstorm with the possibility of a tornado, she reminded herself.

"Oh, hell…"

She hurried into her office and took a water bottle from the small fridge, then went into her storage room, resisting the urge to close the door and shut out the storm. Boxes were piled haphazardly on one side. On the other, shelves were neatly labeled…and empty. She'd been putting it off…might as well use this time to organize her inventory. She tried to ignore the rumble of thunder and the sound of the oak tree in the back alley brushing against the building as the wind whipped it around.

* * *

"Damn…that sounded close."

Megan stood at the window in their office, looking down the sidewalk to Ruby's. She'd actually flinched as lightning—and the immediate crash of thunder—flashed across the window. The lights flickered a few times, then held steady. She wondered how Leah was faring.

She turned from the window, glancing at Nancy. Now was as good a time as any for a chat. There would be no lunch crowd until the rain let up. The few people who'd made it inside were already taken care of.

"So…what's going on?" she asked obliquely.

"What do you mean?"

"I mean, in a few weeks' time, Mary Beth has gone from showing me a photo on her phone…a photo of me, completely naked, a photo she hinted that she would post…to nothing. Nothing. No stalking. No veiled threats. Nothing," she said again.

"You should be happy."

"Oh, I am. I'm thrilled." She narrowed her eyes. "So what's going on?"

"What makes you think I know something?"

"Because you've been acting weird," she said, pointing her finger at her. "And Mary Beth has been acting weird. Well, weirder than normal. Then it hit me…you've been acting weird *together*," she said knowingly, pleased that Nancy actually blushed.

"I don't know what you're talking about."

Megan stared, her eyes widening. "Oh, my God! *Really?* You and Mary Beth?"

Nancy stood up, pacing behind the desk. "What is it that you're insinuating?"

"I'm insinuating that you and Mary Beth are seeing each other," she said bluntly.

Nancy stopped and her expression turned serious. "And… what if we are?"

"Mary Beth Sturgeon? The woman who stripped me naked and took pictures of me? The woman who posted them on Facebook in an attempt to blackmail me into a date?" She put her hands on her hips. "Are you *serious*?"

Nancy turned on her. "Look, this is all your fault!"

"*My* fault?"

"Yes! You insisted I talk to her, to get her to stop with the Facebook thing. So I did. We started talking…and…well, the next thing I know…"

"Oh, my God! Are you *sleeping* with her?"

Nancy's face turned bright red. "That…is none of your business," she said curtly and brushed past her out of the office.

Megan stood there in shock. She'd convinced herself that she'd imagined the looks that had passed between Nancy and Mary Beth. Apparently not. Apparently her sister was sleeping with freakin' Mary Beth Sturgeon!

"She has lost her mind," she murmured.

CHAPTER THIRTY-FIVE

Leah actually let out a startled scream as the loud crack of thunder seemed to rattle the entire building. Seconds later, the room was plunged into darkness, leaving her scrambling for her phone—and its built-in flashlight.

"Sure…take shelter in a windowless room," she murmured as she held her phone up. She went back out into the shop where the large front windows let in enough light for her to pocket her phone again.

The sky was lightening up and the rain had lessened to a drizzle, but thunder still rumbled. She looked up, staring at the lights, as if expecting them to come back on at any second. She wondered what the norm was around here for power outages. An hour? Half a day? Several days?

She walked over to the door and opened it, finding others standing under cover, looking around and talking. The whole street was dark…maybe the whole town. She turned, glancing at the Phenix Grill. She could always dash over there. She was about to do that when another flash of lightning and clap of thunder sent her back inside. So maybe later.

Besides, she figured she needed to give Megan some time. They'd left things kinda up in the air last night. Knowing Megan, she had settled on the "it was a terrible idea" for them to date theme. And when she was ready, she'd come over and tell Leah so.

But when they were together, there was that underlying attraction that seemed to pull at them. Common sense seemed to go right out the window then...for both of them. Why else were they in this position to begin with? *Fake* dating? Whose idea was that, anyway?

"I believe it was *yours*," she murmured.

* * *

Megan stood at the window, indecisive. She was certain Leah was okay. Why wouldn't she be? It was only a power outage, a common occurrence during spring thunderstorms. But a first for this year...and a first for Leah.

"Go over there already," Nancy said. "There's nothing you can do here."

"What did Paul say?"

"Lightning took out some transformers. Power is out pretty much all over up here. They still have power down the hill though."

"Well, I guess I could go check on her," she said with a shrug.

Nancy waved her away. "I won't worry about you."

The rain was only a few sprinkles now, but Megan still heard thunder off to the east. She looked up, noting the dark clouds drifting away and, farther west, blue skies beginning to show. The door to Ruby's was closed, and she wouldn't have been surprised to find it locked as well. However, it opened easily and she went inside.

"Leah?"

The shop turned dark and shadowy when she moved away from the windows. She went to the back where Leah's office was.

"Leah?" she called again.

She heard shuffling in the storage room, finally seeing a tiny beam of light. Leah was sifting through a box.

"Hey."

Leah jumped, startled, and dropped her phone. "Jesus! You scared me!"

"Sorry," she said as Leah bent down and picked up her phone again. "What are you doing?"

"Looking for a damn flashlight. Or matches."

"Matches? Are you going to burn boxes or something?"

"No. I have candles." She paused. "Somewhere."

"So you have no emergency kit?"

"Well, if I was still in San Jose I'd have one...for an earthquake."

Megan laughed. "I don't imagine you'll need that here. Tornado, maybe, but no earthquake."

Leah moved closer to her. "I don't mind saying, I was a little scared. I'm not exactly used to thunderstorms like that."

Megan shrugged. "I guess I've seen so many, they don't really bother me. Lightning hit a transformer, by the way. Or two." She reached in her back pocket and pulled out the small flashlight. "And I'm prepared," she said as she turned it on.

"Flashlights, extra batteries. On my shopping list."

"Oh, and you should probably lock your door," Megan said, motioning out into the shop. "I could have stolen you blind earlier."

"You would have attempted to steal those expensive wind chimes that you play with whenever you come in," Leah said. "I would have heard you and caught you red-handed!"

"Oh, yeah?"

Leah took a step closer. "Uh-huh."

It should have been nothing, Megan thought. They were playing, teasing. She'd come over to talk, hadn't she? Her mistake, of course, was looking into Leah's eyes. The flashlight, though small, was strong enough to create a halo around the two of them. Those dark, smoky eyes held hers, and Megan found herself moving toward Leah as if she were under a hypnotic spell. Who reached who first, she didn't know…she didn't care. She found herself being held against the shelves, Leah's body pressed so closely to hers, she could feel every inch of her.

Their kisses were wild—mouths, lips, tongues attacking without thought. She never thought she could be delirious from a kiss, but Leah, with her hands sliding up her body, had driven her into such a fevered state that she felt weak…faint.

Then Leah slowed their kisses, her lips moving to Megan's neck, nibbling softly as Megan's hands wound around her waist.

"You smell…taste…so good," Leah murmured.

If Megan could have held onto a cognizant thought, she would have replied—something witty, no doubt. But her brain was a jumbled mess, and she was just thankful her knees hadn't buckled. She managed a loud moan, a moan that seemed to strike fire in Leah as her mouth came back to hers, kissing her again with such passion it made Megan lightheaded and she had to hold on to Leah for fear she'd actually fall. Somewhere in her muddled mind, she knew they should stop. Her body, however, ignored that thought, and when Leah nudged her thighs apart with her leg, Megan moaned again as Leah pressed hard against her. They were close…dangerously close…to reaching the point of no return. She found she didn't care.

But, alas, it was not to be.

"Hello?" a loud voice called from the shop. "Are you open?"

"Oh, God," Megan groaned. "Are you *kidding* me?"

"Yeah…be right there," Leah called back, her voice still breathless from their kissing. "I've got to get a bell for that damn door," she murmured.

"How about a lock?"

Leah laughed quietly as she stepped away from Megan. "Go upstairs," she said quietly. "I have candles. Somewhere." Then she smiled. "Feel free to snoop around looking for them."

Megan swallowed. This was her out. She could say no. She could leave. Because if she stayed...

One look into Leah's eyes, however, made any thoughts of leaving vanish. There was such desire there, she was certain she'd never seen anyone look at her that way before. There was no way she could leave. She moved closer instead, kissing Leah again...and again, she just wanted to rip their clothes off and get naked.

Leah thankfully came to her senses and pushed Megan gently away from her.

"You drive me crazy," Megan whispered.

"Yeah...and again, I hope that's a good thing."

She turned and left Megan standing there in the dark. She looked around, finding the flashlight lying at her feet. She had no recollection of dropping it. She took several deep breaths, then left the storage room, ignoring the muted voices she heard from the shop. She hurried up the stairs and into Leah's apartment.

CHAPTER THIRTY-SIX

Leah tapped the counter impatiently as the two women sorted through the T-shirts. As she'd told them, she couldn't sell anything until the power came back on. She had hoped they'd simply leave. But no. They wanted to look around and decide if it was worth coming back at another time.

"Oh, these sound beautiful," one said as she put the chimes in motion.

"Yes, they're my favorites," Leah said, watching as the woman looked at the price.

"Oh, my."

Leah smiled, then walked over. "They're handcrafted, that's why they cost more," she explained. "These are a little cheaper here," she said, pointing to the chimes hanging on the lower level of the rack.

"Yes, much more reasonable."

You get what you pay for, Leah thought as she moved back toward the counter, trying not to glance at the clock above her head. If she wanted Ruby's to be a success, she needed to be patient with potential customers, even when they were shopping, knowing they were unable to buy a thing. But making Ruby's a success right now wasn't what was foremost on her mind. Foremost on her mind was the woman waiting for her upstairs. She closed her eyes for a moment, still feeling the heat between them. God, what would it be like in bed? Naked… skin on skin…she could imagine the fire. She opened her eyes again. She didn't want to imagine it. She wanted to *feel* it.

So she cleared her throat rather loudly. "I'm thinking I'm going to go ahead and close up shop," she called to the women who were on the other side of the store. "Doesn't look like the power will be back on any time soon."

"You have a lot of interesting things here," one said, holding up a wood carving of an eagle. "There's a shop in town that sells woodworking, but their stuff is rather cheap looking."

"Thank you. Perhaps you'd like to come back tomorrow," she suggested. "I'm sure the power will be back on by then."

She put the eagle down. "Yes, I think we'll be back."

"Great," she said, trying not to push them out the door. "I'll see you tomorrow then."

As soon as they were out, she locked the door and flipped over the sign in the window to "closed." She nearly took the stairs two at a time, then slowed, pausing to catch her breath.

"I hope she hasn't changed her mind," she murmured as she opened the door.

* * *

Megan's hand was trembling as she struck the match—trembling so badly the match went out. What in the hell was she doing here in Leah's bedroom…lighting candles, no less? She knew what was going to happen. Of course she did. She wasn't going to pretend that she hadn't seen that look in Leah's eyes. She wasn't going to pretend that she was innocent in this. There was no sense in pretending that she didn't want to make love with Leah. She did. Desperately so, if her actions in the storage room were any indication. But there was no more time to contemplate it. She heard the door open and she looked out from the bedroom, seeing Leah enter the apartment. Leah glanced around quickly, then her eyes were drawn to the bedroom and she walked toward it. Megan's heart hammered nervously, and she tried once again to light the candle. With her hand still trembling, she managed to touch the wick, the light brightening the room somewhat.

She turned slowly, finding Leah standing in the doorway, still hidden by shadows. Megan's pulse was beating rapidly and she felt as nervous as a virgin might feel on her wedding night. But she wasn't an innocent girl, and this wasn't her wedding night. There was absolutely nothing to be nervous about. Still…she couldn't seem to find her voice so she stood there mutely, watching as Leah finally walked into the bedroom.

She wondered if Leah was as nervous as she was. She, too, kept quiet as they stood there watching each other. In the shadows, she couldn't read Leah's eyes, but she didn't have to.

The hand that reached out to her was shaking slightly. The sight of Leah's nervousness eased her own somewhat.

There were no words between them, and the only sound in the room was their breathing, louder, more labored than it should be. When Leah undid the top button on her blouse, her fingers brushed Megan's skin, causing her to suck in a quick breath. She stood still—waiting—as Leah moved to the next button. Slowly, one by one, the buttons gave way, exposing her. When her blouse finally fell open, Leah's fingertips grazed the fabric of her black bra, moving under the swell of one breast, then the other before teasing the skin between them. Goosebumps traveled up and down her skin, and Megan felt her knees begin to shake. She was afraid she'd fall, afraid she'd melt right there where she stood.

Leah's gaze was following the progress of her fingers, but when she scraped her index finger against a nipple, she lifted her head, locking Megan's eyes with her dark, smoky ones.

Megan tried to swallow, but she couldn't. She was having a hard enough time breathing as it was. And if Leah didn't rip her bra off within the next few seconds, Megan would likely do it herself. She literally ached to feel Leah's hands on her skin, on her breasts, on her body.

The blouse was pushed off her shoulders, and Megan let it fall to the ground. Her lips were parted slightly as she drew uneven breaths, her gaze still holding fast to Leah's. One strap of her bra was lowered so agonizingly slowly that Megan was on the verge of begging Leah to hurry. Instead, she bit her lower lip, waiting, as Leah took her time, finally reaching for the other strap. Instead of removing her bra, she left the straps halfway down, her fingers tracing along the edge of the bra, lightly touching her breast. Again, Megan drew in a sharp breath as a fingertip brushed her nipple.

Seconds turned into minutes as Leah finally, mercifully, unfastened her bra. Megan nearly flung it across the room, so ready to have Leah's hands on her. But again, Leah took her time, moving closer, her lips starting along Megan's jawline, traveling slowly across her face to her lips. By the time Leah's mouth found hers, Megan was on the verge of bursting into flames. She clutched Leah to her, actually shocked that she still had the strength to stand. Conscious thought, however, failed her as primal urges took over.

Megan's hands tugged at Leah's shirt. They parted long enough for her to pull it over Leah's head, then mouths and tongues reunited as Megan fumbled with Leah's bra. Clothes fell on the floor around them, then Leah pulled the covers back on the bed and urged Megan down with her.

Skin touching skin, hot and slick…mouths still fighting for control, Leah rolled them over, resting on top of Megan and nudging Megan's legs apart. Megan groaned as Leah's thigh was pressed hard against her. Her hips jerked up to meet her, her hands cupping Leah, pulling her even tighter.

But Leah wouldn't be rushed. Her mouth left Megan's, moving lower, a wet tongue bathing her breast, finally raking against her nipple. Megan's eyes slammed closed as that hot mouth surrounded her nipple, sucking it inside, Leah's tongue swirling around it, making it rock-hard. Her hips jerked again, the fire inside her too hot to stand any longer. Her legs parted even farther and she could feel her wetness as it coated Leah's thigh.

"Please," she whispered, the first word spoken between them.

Leah rocked her thigh against her, rubbing against her clit. Megan was panting now, holding on tightly to Leah as their hips banged together. Leah's mouth left her breast, coming back to hers, their tongues dancing again. Megan felt Leah's hand move between them, felt fingers slip into her wetness, teasing her clit. She felt feverish, and she moaned into Leah's mouth when fingers entered her. Leah's strokes were hard, sure, her hips still slamming against Megan with a rhythm that she matched.

When Leah's mouth left hers, going to her ear instead, her tongue dipping inside, her lips whispering words that Megan's muddled mind couldn't decipher—she exploded, her body seemingly breaking into tiny pieces, and a kaleidoscope of colors flashed across her eyes, blinding her, causing her to scream out in pleasure as her hips rose one last time, keeping Leah deep within her for a precious few seconds longer.

She collapsed then, falling back onto the bed, her arms dropping uselessly to either side of her, her eyes still closed, her lips parted, drawing in quick breaths. She felt Leah's lips as they nibbled—first her neck, down to her breasts, against her stomach, the curve of her hip, then slowly made the return trip back to her mouth.

Megan moaned with contentment as they kissed and she gathered Leah close against her, holding her tightly. God, how different was this than being with Erin? *Night and day*, she mused. Who would have thought that an older woman could rock her world like Leah just had?

"That was...unbelievable," she murmured, moving to kiss Leah again. The fire still burned, and she felt Leah shift, rolling over and pulling Megan on top of her. "I hope the power stays out for hours."

Leah opened her legs and Megan slipped between them. "You and me both," Leah said as Megan's lips trailed down her neck to her breasts.

As her tongue swirled around Leah's nipple, as she heard the quiet moan that Leah let escape, she thought that yes, she could indeed stay here for hours...making love. As she drew Leah's nipple into her mouth, her own moan mingled with Leah's. Her fingers moved along Leah's skin, feeling her tremble. Yes, she would take her time. There was no need to rush. They had all afternoon if they wanted.

And she wanted. Oh...she so *wanted*.

CHAPTER THIRTY-SEVEN

Megan should be exhausted. Okay...she *was* exhausted. But she felt invigorated, fresh...new. She had no idea what time the power had come back on. She had no idea what time she got home. She had no idea how many hours she slept. Yet this morning, she felt energized. The sun was shining a little brighter, the sky was a little bluer, the coffee more aromatic.

She leaned against the counter, taking her first sip. It was wonderful. *Everything* was wonderful. Who knew spending an afternoon and most of the night with Leah Rollins would have this effect on her?

And God, what an afternoon and night it was. She was surprised she could even walk this morning. That thought brought a smile to her face as she remembered a particular instance where she thought she'd pulled her hamstring. Her smile widened as she took another sip. What an absolutely glorious day it had been.

Her smile faltered a little. Now what? Where did they go from here? Were they a couple now? For real? The terrible idea of them dating didn't seem so terrible right now. In fact, it seemed quite the opposite of terrible. The scary part was… as great as the sex had been, it was the times between the sex that made her heart get all warm and fuzzy. They'd cuddled, they'd talked, they'd laughed…and then they'd made love all over again.

It was all almost *too* perfect. She frowned. So obviously something was *very* wrong. This didn't happen to her. Women like Leah didn't happen to her…women like Tammi and Erin did. That was her track record. Not Leah.

"Well…I see you did make it home," Nancy said as she reached for her coffee cup. She glanced at her, her eyes widening. "Oh, my God! You've had sex!"

Megan felt a blush light her face. "Must you do that?"

Nancy laughed. "You're glowing."

"I am not glowing."

"Oh, you are *so* glowing." Nancy grinned. "Was it good?"

Megan couldn't stop her smile. "It was fabulous."

Nancy clapped her hands together and tapped her feet. "Yay! I'm so happy for you!" Then she stopped. "Does she have toys?" she asked in a near whisper.

"Really? That's what you want to know?" She shook her head. "Trust me, she didn't need toys."

Nancy smirked. "Mary Beth has toys."

Megan shook her head. "Now why doesn't *that* surprise me?" When Nancy's statement finally registered, though, her eyes widened. "Wait a minute. So you and Mary Beth really *are* having sex?"

"We are."

Megan had to bite her tongue to prevent her "You have lost your freakin' mind!" reply from popping out. "That's…that's great," she said instead.

Nancy's smile was genuine. "Yes, it is. I've gotten to see a side of her that, well, that she hasn't shown us in all the years we've lived here. She's like a completely different person."

"So the whole naked pictures thing, the Facebook stalking, the stealing and wearing my bra…that was all someone else?"

Nancy laughed. "Speaking of that…" She left the kitchen only to return a few moments later, swinging a red bra around on her index finger. "I believe this is yours."

Megan snatched it out of her hands, then held it up in Nancy's face. "She *stole* my favorite bra and then had the nerve to *wear* it!" She made a face. "Please say she didn't wear this when you had sex."

Nancy rolled her eyes. "As usual, you're being too dramatic. She wore it the one time, just to get a rise out of you."

"Oh, my God," Megan murmured as she grabbed the bridge of her nose. "I can't believe you're *sleeping* with her."

"Well, believe it. I…" she paused. "I like her, Megan."

All of Mary Beth's ramblings on falling in love came back to her, and she groaned silently. Surely to God Nancy wasn't *falling* for Mary Beth Sturgeon! Well, it wasn't any of her business. She had gotten her bra back. And as far as she knew, Mary Beth had ceased posting naked pictures of her. If Nancy wanted to be involved with a crazy woman, who was she to say otherwise?

"If you like her, that's all that matters," Megan said diplomatically.

"Thank you. And by the way, Mom called. They're coming Friday."

"What? *This* Friday? Like tomorrow?"

"Oh, yeah. This is Thursday already, isn't it? They'll be here five days," Nancy said. "They'll have to stay with us. I couldn't get them a room on such short notice."

"This is so unlike them. They usually plan this a month in advance. What's going on?"

"They're taking a road trip. When they leave here, they're heading north. Dad wants to drive to Niagara Falls." Nancy waved her hand in the air. "Mom is not crazy about it, but Dad supposedly has the whole trip planned."

"Where are they going to sleep?"

"You're the youngest. I think you should take the sofa and give them your bed."

"For five nights? I think we should take turns." Then she smiled. "Or I could maybe stay with Leah."

Nancy grinned. "I'm sure I could find a place to stay too. We'll flip for it!"

CHAPTER THIRTY-EIGHT

Leah brushed Megan's nipple with her finger, circling it, watching as it hardened. She decided that Megan had perfect breasts. Full, firm…delicious. She looked up as Megan ran her fingers through her hair slowly.

"I love your hair," Megan murmured. "It matches your eyes."

Leah leaned closer, kissing Megan's nipple, then scooted up higher in the bed next to her. She loved Megan's voice after they made love. It was still thick with emotion, soft yet heavy.

"I love your breasts," she countered.

"I love your mouth on my breasts," Megan said as she leaned over for a kiss. "In fact, I love your mouth in a *lot* of places."

Leah smiled. "I could tell."

Megan sighed and snuggled against her. "What a perfect afternoon," she said. "Aren't you glad you hired Aunt Dee?"

"I am so happy I hired Dee. Especially if you're going to make a habit of sneaking over here like this."

"We had a lull between the lunch crowd and dinner," Megan said. "And I really, really wanted to kiss you."

"This from the woman who said there would be no kissing," she reminded her.

"I believe I allowed fake kissing."

"Well, for your information, none of them were fake. I only said they were to appease you."

Megan laughed. "Well, now, aren't you the sneaky one."

Leah leaned up on her elbow and rested her face in her palm. With her other hand, she absently rubbed circles on Megan's stomach. She was smiling and she couldn't seem to stop. As Megan had said, what a perfectly wonderful afternoon it was. She could *so* get used to this.

"By the way, my parents are coming into town tomorrow," Megan said.

"Oh, yeah? Do I get to meet them?"

"Yes. Nancy is planning a Sunday afternoon party at our place. You'll never guess what she wants to serve."

Leah laughed. "Hamburgers?"

"Yes! Freakin' hamburgers on the grill. She's having Johnny season them up ahead of time so all she had to do is cook them." Megan rolled toward to her. "And you'll never believe this. Nancy and Mary Beth are *sleeping* together! I still can't wrap my mind around it. It's too creepy to think about."

"Well, they were quite chummy at our dinner party the other night."

"I know. So it wasn't a complete shock…but still."

"Is she happy?"

Megan nodded. "Yes, and that's all that should matter, I know."

"Right." Leah rolled to her back and pulled Megan with her. "And are you happy?"

Megan's expression turned serious. "I'm almost *too* happy," she whispered. "If I happen to fall in love with you, would you please not break my heart?"

Leah was the one who felt too happy. Years ago she had given up on finding someone to share her life with. She had resolved to be alone. She'd accepted it and was content. Hell, she was over fifty. At what point do you admit to yourself that you're not going to meet the love of your life?

But then something wonderful happened. A fiery, grumpy, beautiful young woman walked into her shop and threw a wadded up note in her face. She smiled, remembering their first encounter. She should have recognized it then. Megan had stolen her heart that very day.

Leah reversed their positions, resting her weight on top of Megan now. "If you happen to fall in love with me, I wouldn't *dare* break your heart."

"You promise?"

Leah kissed her gently. "I *so* promise."

CHAPTER THIRTY-NINE

"I'm surprised you can both be away from the grill at the same time," her mother said.

"On Sundays, lunch is the busiest," Megan said. "I covered that while Nancy got things ready here. Eileen is handling dinner."

"She needs a raise, by the way," Nancy said. "We've been relying on her for so much lately. It's not like you and I are there constantly anymore."

"You're not? Why?" their mother asked.

"Oh...you know," Megan said vaguely as she and Nancy exchanged glances.

They had decided not to tell their mother about Leah and Mary Beth. At least not yet. Although since both Leah and Mary Beth were coming over, she didn't think they'd be able to keep it from their mother. Megan was likely to turn into a puddle of goo when Leah got there, and God only knew what Nancy would do with Mary Beth.

Her mother eyed them suspiciously. "You girls have been acting very strange," she said. She turned her attention to Nancy. "And who's this mysterious friend that you're staying with? Not that I don't appreciate your bed," she added.

Megan looked at Nancy with raised eyebrows. They had indeed flipped a coin to see who would give up their bed. Megan had lost, thus being forced to keep her bed and share the house with her parents. Nancy had done a fist pump and promptly packed clothes for a five-day stay with Mary Beth.

"Nothing mysterious about her," Nancy said. "She's coming over later. You'll get to see her then." She handed their mother a knife and a tomato. "I could use a little help."

Their mother glanced at Megan. "There's room for all three of us in the kitchen," she said. "It'll be like old times."

Megan held her hands up and backed away. "I don't do kitchen prep."

"You own a restaurant, for God's sake. Do you still make Nancy do kitchen duty?"

"We've settled on a routine, yes."

"So you always get bar duty?"

Megan smiled. "I've turned into a pretty good bartender, thank you very much."

She had just gone outside to sit with her father when the doorbell rang. She immediately felt her pulse quicken with nervousness as she went back inside to get the door. Would it be Leah? She hadn't seen her since their afternoon together. Their parents had gotten there earlier on Friday than they'd expected and had simply stayed at the grill until closing. Yesterday, Saturday, it was too busy for her to even think about going over to Ruby's for a visit. She had peeked over there a few times, though, and noticed that Leah had customers. She hoped she'd been as busy as they were at the grill.

It was not Leah, however, at the door. It was Mary Beth, holding a bottle of wine. Megan stared at her for a few seconds. She looked different. Had she lost weight? Her hair had been trimmed, she knew that much.

"Hello, Megan."

"Mary Beth," she said in as friendly a tone as she could manage. "Come in."

"Am I early?"

"No. Nancy's in the kitchen," she said, stepping aside to let Mary Beth enter. Mary Beth paused, as if she wanted to say something. Megan raised her eyebrows questioningly.

"Well, I…" Mary Beth glanced toward the kitchen. "I need to apologize to you," she said. "The whole Facebook thing."

"Do you mean for stripping me naked against my will and taking pictures of me? Or for actually *posting* those pictures?" she asked pointedly, glad to see Mary Beth look uncomfortable about the situation. It was about time.

"Both, of course," Mary Beth said. "I…I don't have an excuse, other than stupidity."

"Nancy insisted that it was all in fun, but you and I know that wasn't the case. Was it?"

"No. As I said, it was a stupid attempt to get you to go out with me. I'm truly sorry. I've removed the photos, I've deleted them. I—"

"The one you showed me on your phone?"

"Yes, that too."

Megan narrowed her eyes. "And of course you've deleted them all from your memory as well?"

"Oh, absolutely."

Megan finally smiled. "Thank you. I suppose Nancy had something to do with that?"

"I told you before—sometimes love is right under your nose. I've been quite charmed by your sister. We've become close this last month, and I don't only mean physically."

Megan held her hand up. "I don't need details. And she seems very happy."

"We both are."

"Then we can say something good came of this." She paused. "Actually, I suppose I should thank you, as crazy as that sounds. In a roundabout way, it was because of you that Leah and I started dating in the first place."

"What do you mean?"

Oh, crap. Mary Beth didn't need to know about their silly fake dating plan. *No* one needed to *ever* know about it! "I mean, I needed someone to talk to, someone to turn to," she said, which wasn't a lie. "I needed an ally. Nancy had become yours. Anyway, it brought Leah and me together. And as you said, we've become really close in the last month." She grinned. "And I don't just mean physically."

Mary Beth laughed. "Well, glad that crazy plan of mine helped push things along." She shrugged. "So you forgive me?"

Megan nodded. "I forgive you." She pointed toward the kitchen. "Nancy's in there with our mom."

Mary Beth held up the wine bottle. "This is actually for you and Leah. It's that red zinfandel that you liked. Leah is coming, right?"

"That was nice of you, thanks. And yes, she's coming." As if on cue, the doorbell rang.

"I'll drop this off in the kitchen," Mary Beth said.

Megan nodded, but her attention was already on the door. She opened it, finding Leah standing there. The dark shirt she was wearing made her eyes look smoky blue today. Megan fell into them as quickly as she fell into her arms. Had it only been two days since she'd seen her?

Kissing someone on her front porch was a first for Megan, and she did temper her greeting somewhat because of that. However, the kiss was enough to bring back all sorts of delicious memories, and she allowed herself to press tightly against Leah's body.

"I missed you," Leah murmured into her ear as she held her close. "How many more days until your parents leave?"

"Three more nights." She pulled away, smiling. "I was planning an elaborate escape through my window and a quick jog down the hill to Ruby's, but I decided it would be easier to simply tell them the truth." She met Leah's eyes, her voice lowering to nearly a whisper. "I want to sleep there tonight. I want to be with you."

Leah met her gaze, smiling. "I would love for you to sleep with me tonight. I'll treat you to a special breakfast."

"You, naked in bed, is treat enough."

Leah laughed. "I'll wear a sexy apron while I cook," she tempted.

"Oh, now that's a visual," Megan said. She linked arms with Leah and led her inside. "Come, meet my parents."

CHAPTER FORTY

"Isn't she the one you called arrogant?"

Megan nodded. "Yes."

"And annoying? And a bully?"

"Yes."

"And the spawn of Satan?"

"Yes, Mom."

"And now you're dating?"

"Well...it's complicated."

"She's very attractive. Mature. Polite. I only met Erin the one time," she said. "She was an immature child. Cute, but a child. And of course you know how I felt about Tammi."

Megan held her hand up. "We don't need to rehash my past failures, Mom." Then she smiled. "I really like her though. I...I think I could fall in love with her."

Her mom hugged her quickly. "Honey, I saw the way you looked at her. I think you already have."

"It...it feels different. I feel different."

"You look different too. Happy. I haven't seen you look happy in so long, Megan. It's nice to see a spark in your eyes."

"Yes. Maybe that's what feels different. I feel happy," she said with a smile. And that was true. She felt like singing, like laughing, like dancing in the rain. "It feels good, Mom."

Her mother hugged her again. "Yes, it does." When they pulled apart, her mother was smiling. "So…what's with Nancy and Mary Beth?"

Megan feigned ignorance. "What do you mean?"

"Isn't this the Mary Beth who was posting pictures of you?"

"Yes, the same."

"Trying to blackmail you into a date, right?"

Megan nodded. "Yes."

"So? What's going on?"

Megan shrugged. "They're friends."

"Oh, please. Nancy is practically giddy."

Megan smiled. "Yes, she is. Scary, isn't it?"

"So they *are* dating?" her mother asked in a whisper.

"I'm afraid so."

Her mother shook her head. "I'll never be able to explain all of this to your father."

* * *

Leah had just shoved a chip loaded with sour cream dip into her mouth when she saw Mrs. Phenix make her way over to her. She smiled apologetically as she chewed.

"Sorry…I love sour cream and this dip is wonderful," she said.

"Thank you. It's my secret recipe." She leaned closer. "The girls have been badgering me for years to give it to them," she said quietly. "If I did that, then they'd make it all the time and it would no longer be special."

Leah took another sample. "Shrimp, obviously. Cream cheese mixed with sour cream?"

Mrs. Phenix nodded. "Yes. The girls have tried to duplicate it on their own, but they always miss one or two key ingredients." She smiled. "I suppose one day I'll have to give it up."

"Well, if I promise to keep it a secret, would you pass it on to me?"

"Seeing as how you're sleeping with my daughter, I'm not sure how many secrets there would be."

Leah was surprised at how easily that statement made her blush. She didn't expect Mrs. Phenix to be that direct, although she shouldn't have been surprised, not after knowing both Megan and Nancy.

Mrs. Phenix laughed. "Sorry. I shouldn't have been so blunt. Megan seems quite fond of you."

Leah nodded. "I hope so. Because I'm very fond of her."

"I assume you know about Tammi? And Erin?"

"I know that they both cheated on her. Is that what you mean?"

She nodded. "Yes. I don't believe Megan was all that invested in Erin, but she and Tammi shared a house. Megan was devastated." She leaned closer, her voice quiet. "Do you know about the fire?"

Leah managed to suppress a smile. "Nancy mentioned it a while back, before Leah and I were dating."

Mrs. Phenix laughed. "And you *still* went out with Megan?"

"Well, Nancy didn't really go into details. Are you suggesting I need to get all the facts first?"

She was surprised by Mrs. Phenix's hand wrapping around her arm and squeezing tightly. "I think it's too late for that, don't you? Too late for both of you."

Leah met her gaze and nodded. "Yes. It is too late."

The hand slipped from her arm. "I could tell. Megan looks as happy as I've ever seen her." Her expression turned serious. "May I offer a bit of advice?"

"Please."

"Don't keep secrets of any kind. Communication is the key to a successful relationship, Leah. Communication and honesty. There'll always be disagreements, of course. That's a given. And I'm sure you already know that Megan can be a little…well, difficult."

Leah laughed. "Difficult? Is that a nice way of saying temperamental?"

"Let's just hope you don't do anything to cause her to start a fire and toss your belongings into it." She laughed. "What a sight that was!"

"Oh. My. *God!* Say you are *not* telling her about that!"

They turned to find Megan glaring at them. Leah couldn't hide her smile, and Mrs. Phenix waved her hand dismissively.

"She has a right to know what will happen if she cheats on you, doesn't she?"

Megan covered her face with both hands. "Please say you didn't tell her, Mother."

Mrs. Phenix glanced at Leah. "She only calls me Mother when I'm in trouble," she murmured. Then she turned to Megan. "I didn't tell her. Nancy did."

Megan's eyes flew to Leah's. "You already knew about it?"

Leah nodded. "Yeah. I hear you made the paper."

Megan groaned. "I'll kill her."

"I think it's classic," Leah said with a laugh. "How many people have thought about doing that?" She laughed again. "And on Halloween. I have an image of you in a witch's costume, hauling her stuff outside and piling it on the fire."

Mrs. Phenix laughed too. "I still have the newspaper clipping."

"Mom…*please*," Megan groaned.

"Oh, the article was hilarious. Everyone was talking about it."

"Enough." Megan grabbed Leah's arm and led her away.

Leah was surprised when they went past the kitchen and into the other side of the house. Megan opened a door and pulled Leah into a bedroom, closing the door behind them. Leah glanced around the room—the bed neatly made, the blinds open to let in the sun, the dresser impeccably tidy.

"I…I should explain," Megan said.

"You don't have to explain."

"You must think I'm a little nuts. I mean, the police—"

"I know. The fire department and police both showed up. You made the paper. The neighbors thought you were crazy."

Megan stared at her. "I can't *believe* she told you."

Leah smiled. "She did preface it by saying you'd kill her if you found out."

"I was...I was so angry, so humiliated. And she was laughing about it. Bragging about how long she'd gotten away with cheating on me. I...I snapped," Megan said. "I started throwing her things out on the lawn and we're screaming at each other and yes, the neighbors were starting to gather."

"And the fire?"

"We had those damn Tiki torches with the oil in them. They were hideous. If they'd been the wicker or bamboo or whatever it is, fine. But these were gaudy colored with faces painted on them. And if we lived near a beach, okay. Even a pool. But in a neighborhood in St. Louis?" Megan shook her head. "Anyway, I was glad to be rid of them. Tammi went berserk when the oil spilled out onto her clothes. And I guess I went berserk when I tossed a match on it."

"So she called the police?"

"Yes. And a neighbor called the fire department." Megan covered her face. "It was a mess. I was so embarrassed. I had to move. None of the neighbors would speak to me after that."

Leah moved closer, taking her hand. "You're a passionate woman, Megan. There's nothing wrong with that."

Megan met her gaze. "Passionate or not, I should have never set her things on fire. That's really bothered me all these years. I tried to apologize, but she wouldn't see me, wouldn't talk to me."

"That's when you left St. Louis and moved here?"

"Yes."

"Well, then I guess I should be happy you started the fire. We would never have met otherwise."

Megan finally smiled. "That's the rationale we should use?"

Leah nodded. "It works for me. And if you're wondering if I think you're dangerous or not...well, I think you're very, very dangerous." She pulled her closer. "For completely different reasons, of course."

Megan settled against her, wrapping her arms tightly around her waist. Leah sighed contentedly as they held each other.

"Mary Beth apologized to me, by the way."

"Did she now?"

Megan's lips nibbled against her neck, causing Leah's eyes to close. "She's in love with my sister," Megan murmured.

Leah turned her head, finding Megan's mouth. The gentleness of their kiss didn't last long, not with their bodies pressed together like they were. One brush of Megan's tongue against hers caused her own fire to start. When she felt Megan's hands slide up to cup her breasts, she moaned and pulled Megan even closer to her.

"If you don't stop, I'm going to lock the door and take you to bed," Leah threatened. She felt Megan smile against her lips.

"Tonight. Your place," Megan whispered.

Leah finally separated from Megan, then leaned closer and kissed her once again. She paused, touching Megan's face with her fingertips, her gaze traveling across smooth skin to find her eyes.

"I'm totally captivated by you, you know."

Megan took her hand and gently kissed her palm, letting her lips linger. "And I'm falling in love with you."

Leah ignored her racing pulse as she moved closer to kiss Megan yet again. "Fall faster," she whispered. "I'll catch you."

Their eyes held for precious seconds, and Megan finally nodded. They smiled at each other, the kind of sickly sweet smiles that new lovers often share. Then, without another word, Megan took her hand and led her out of the room.

Laughter was coming from the kitchen, and Leah squeezed her hand as they headed toward it. But just before they got there, Megan stopped and turned, a smile still playing on her lips.

"Have we talked lately about me getting my parking spot back?"

Leah laughed. "*My* parking spot," she corrected.

"A good girlfriend would let me park there," Megan countered.

"I knew that was the only reason you were dating me."

"Well, there are a couple of other reasons," Megan teased. "Should I name them?"

"Maybe tonight. When we're naked."

Megan's eyes softened. "I vote we eat and run."

"Yeah? Suits me fine."

"They'll all know why we're leaving, of course."

"Of course."

"Will that bother you?"

"Not in the least. And by the looks Mary Beth and Nancy have been exchanging, they may beat us to it."

Megan grinned. "Then eat fast."

*　*　*

Megan rested her head on her elbow, her other hand moving aimlessly across Leah's skin, feeling Leah tremble when she touched a particularly sensitive spot.

"Are you happy?"

Megan looked up, smiling at Leah's whispered question. "Inside…inside, I don't think I've ever felt this happy before." She met Leah's gaze. "More ecstatic than happy." She arched an eyebrow, flipping the question to Leah. "You?"

Leah nodded. "Beyond happy…wherever that place is."

Megan leaned down, brushing her lips across Leah's. "Yeah. I'm in that place too."

Leah pulled her closer, and Megan snuggled against her, sighing contentedly. Was it too soon to be feeling this way? Was she falling too hard, too fast? Probably. It didn't matter though. It wasn't like she could stop. Not now. Leah had touched her in a way that no one else ever had. She couldn't explain it, not even to herself. All she knew was that when Leah was near, her pulse raced. When Leah kissed her, her knees got weak. And when Leah made love to her, the world began spinning so fast, all Megan could do was to hold on...hold on tightly and pray that Leah would catch her when she fell.

Because, she knew—in her soul—that she had already fallen.

She'd fallen in love with Leah Rollins.

She raised her head slightly, finding Leah's eyes on her, those smoky blue eyes that she knew she could trust...trust with her life, trust with her love. She didn't need the fluttering of her heart to tell her what she saw there. Leah's eyes were open to her.

Leah had fallen too.

"I'll catch you," Megan whispered.

Leah smiled...an easy, gentle smile that nearly melted Megan's heart.

"Good. Because I'm free falling right now."

Megan leaned closer, kissing Leah as tenderly as she could, hearing Leah's soft moan as she pulled away.

"Fair warning," she said. "If I catch you, I'm not ever letting you go."

"Consider me warned." Then Leah smiled and rolled them over, resting her weight on top of Megan. "Just remember, it won't matter what you do, how much you beg and plead or threaten...you're not getting your parking space back."

Megan laughed. "We'll see about that."

Bella Books, Inc.

Women. Books. Even Better Together.

P.O. Box 10543
Tallahassee, FL 32302

Phone: 800-729-4992
www.bellabooks.com